Cecil Scott Forester was born in Cairo in 1899 and educated at Dulwich College and Guy's Hospital, where he studied medicine. After successfully publishing his first novel, *Payment Deferred*, at the age of twenty-four, he went on to become the author of over forty books which have sold in millions all over the world, and have been translated into many languages. His most popular books are undoubtedly his brilliant military-historical novels, of which the *Hornblower* naval adventures are best known.

Several of his novels have been made into films, including *The African Queen* which, with Humphrey Bogart and Katherine Hepburn in the lead roles, has become a cinema classic. After the war C. S. Forester settled in California, where he lived until his death in 1966.

Also by C. S. Forester

*Novels*
PAYMENT DEFERRED
BROWN ON RESOLUTION
THE GUN
DEATH TO THE FRENCH
THE AFRICAN QUEEN
THE GENERAL
THE EARTHLY PARADISE
THE CAPTAIN FROM CONNECTICUT
THE SHIP
THE SKY AND THE FOREST
RANDALL AND THE RIVER OF TIME
THE NIGHTMARE
THE GOOD SHEPHERD
MR MIDSHIPMAN HORNBLOWER
LIEUTENANT HORNBLOWER
HORNBLOWER AND THE 'HOTSPUR'
HORNBLOWER AND THE CRISIS
HORNBLOWER AND THE 'ATROPOS'
THE HAPPY RETURN
FLYING COLOURS
THE COMMODORE
LORD HORNBLOWER
HORNBLOWER IN THE WEST INDIES

*History*
THE NAVAL WAR OF 1812
HUNTING THE 'BISMARCK'

*Travel*
THE VOYAGE OF THE 'ANNIE MARBLE'
THE 'ANNIE MARBLE' IN GERMANY

*Autobiography*
LONG BEFORE FORTY

*Biography*
NELSON

*Miscellaneous*
MARIONETTES AT HOME
THE HORNBLOWER COMPANION
THE MAN IN THE YELLOW RAFT

*For Children*
POO-POO AND THE DRAGON

# C. S. Forester

# Plain Murder

TRIAD MAYFLOWER

Published in 1978 by Triad/Mayflower Books
Frogmore, St Albans, Herts AL2 2NF

ISBN  0  583  12821  1

Triad Paperbacks Ltd is an imprint of
Chatto, Bodley Head & Jonathan Cape Ltd
and Granada Publishing Ltd

First published by the Bodley Head Ltd 1930

Made and printed in Great Britain by
Hazell Watson & Viney Ltd,
Aylesbury, Bucks
Set in Linotype Times

# CHAPTER I

The three young men sat together at a marble-topped table in the teashop. Their cups of coffee stood untasted before them. The saucer under Reddy's cup was half full of coffee, slopped into it by an irritated waitress who missed the usual familiar smirk which Morris wontedly bestowed upon her when he gave his order. Reddy had not noticed this bad piece of service, although normally it would have curled his fastidious lip. He flicked nervously at the ash of his cigarette and looked across the table at the other two, first Morris with his scowling brow, his woolly hair horrid with grease, his eyelid drooping and his mouth pulled to one side to keep the cigarette smoke out of his eyes, and then Oldroyd with his heavy face wrinkled with perplexity.

'He knows about it all right, then,' said Morris bitterly.

'Certain of it,' said Reddy. 'I couldn't have made a mistake. What would he have said that about Hunter for if he didn't know?'

'It means the sack,' said Oldroyd. 'It does that.'

'Tell me something I don't know,' sneered Morris. 'God damn it, of course it does. We know what Mac's like as well as you do, if not better. The minute he comes back from Glasgow old Harrison'll go trotting in there, and five minutes after that Mac's buzzer will go, and Maudie will come and fetch us in to get the key of the street. Mac won't ever let that by, silly old fool he is, with all his notions about "commercial honour" and stuff like that.'

Morris ended by making a noise in the back of his throat indicating profound disgust; he flung himself back in his chair and filled his lungs deep with cigarette smoke.

'And we'll be looking for a job,' said Oldroyd. 'I've been out before and I know what it's like.'

There was a north-country flavour about his speech: his I's were softened into Ah's.

'Know what it's like? D'you think I don't know too?' said Morris. '"Dear Sir. In reply to your advertisement in today's

*Daily Express*" – bah, I've done hundreds of 'em. God, you're lucky compared to me. I got a wife an' two nippers, don't you forget. An' a fat chance we've got of finding another job. "Copies of two recent testimonials." What sort of testimonials do you think old Mac's going to give us? Sacked for taking bribes! We'll be starving in the streets in a fortnight's time. Jesus, it'll be cold. I've had some. And all I made out of that damned show was three quid – three measly quid, up to date. Just because that blinking fool, Cooper, couldn't keep his mouth shut.'

He glowered round at the other two, and so evident was the fiendish temper which possessed him that they did not dare remind him of the other factors in the situation which oppressed them with grievances beyond the immediate one of prospective dismissal – they dared not remind him that the whole scheme for extracting bribes from Mr Cooper was of his devising, nor that they had only shared three pounds between the two of them; their rogues' agreement gave half the spoils to Morris and divided the other half between Reddy and Oldroyd.

Morris's rage frightened Reddy even more than did the prospect of dismissal; never having been unemployed, and always having had a father and mother at his back, Reddy did not appreciate fully the gnawing fears which were assaulting the other two – hunger and cold were only words to him. Reddy knew his father would be pained and hurt by his ignominious dismissal, but his mother would stand up for him. It might be long before he could buy himself another new suit; it might even mean giving up his beloved motor-bicycle, although such a catastrophe was too stupendous to be really possible; those were realities which lay in the future, while across the table to him was reality in the present – Morris mad with fury, his thick lips writhing round his cigarette and his thick, hairy hands beating on the table.

That may have been Reddy's first contact with reality in all his twenty-two years of life, for that matter. He was in touch with emotions and possibilities which he had only read about, inappreciatively, before that. It was strangely fascinating as well as terrifying. Morris had always exercised a certain fascination for him, possibly through the contrast of his virility and coarseness compared with his own frail elegance, but now in the hour of defeat the spell was stronger still. Certainly at the moment Reddy felt no regret at having allowed Morris to

6

seduce them into the manipulation of correspondence which had left a clear field for the tenders of the Adelphi Artistic Studio, and had earned them six pounds in secret commissions and their approaching dismissal.

The blind ferocity in Morris's face changed suddenly to something more deliberate and calculating.

'By God,' he said, leaning forward and tapping the table, 'if we could get Harrison out of this business it'd be all right for us.'

'How do you mean?' asked Oldroyd blankly.

'I don't know,' said Morris. 'But if we could— Get Mac to fire *him* instead of *us*, or get him out of the way some other way somehow. One of us would get Harrison's job then – eight quid a week, and pickings if you kept your eyes open. And we wouldn't be on the street, either. God! If only we could do it! Can't one of you two dam' fools think of anything?'

'No,' replied Oldroyd, after a blank interval of thought, adding, for the sake of his wilting self-respect, 'And not so much of your dam' fools, either.'

'Dam' fools? Of course we're all dam' fools to be in this blasted mess. But we won't be dam' fools if we get out of it again. Golly, it would be grand if we could!'

'No,' said Oldroyd heavily, 'there isn't any way out. We've just got to take what's coming to us, haven't we, Reddy?'

Reddy nodded, but he was not really in agreement. He was still gazing fascinatedly at Morris's distorted face.

'Don't be a fool and give up the game before you have to,' expostulated Morris, looking sharply round at Oldroyd. 'Mac won't be back at the office until Wednesday. We've still got tomorrow to do something about it. Harrison can't do anything to us on his own. We've still got a chance.'

'Fat lot of chance we've got!' said Oldroyd.

The time which had now elapsed since Reddy had first told the story of his interview with Harrison had given him time to recover some of his fatalistic composure; so much of it, in fact, had returned to him that now he was able to turn his attention to the nearly cold coffee before him. He gulped it down noisily and replaced the cup with a clatter on the saucer. Morris sipped at his.

'God! I can't drink that stuff,' he said, and pushed the cup away.

7

Reddy did not even taste his. Morris looked up at the clock.

'Look at the time! I'll have to bunk to get the 6.20. Give us our tickets, please, miss. So long, you fellows. Keep your pecker up, Oldroyd, old man. We're not dead yet.'

And with that he was gone, forgetting his own exasperation for the moment in the flurry of hurrying out, paying his bill, and scrambling through the traffic in the Strand over to Charing Cross Station. It only returned to him while standing in a packed compartment in the train, crawling along through the first fog of the year; by the time he reached home he was in a bad enough temper to quarrel for the thousandth time with his wife.

## CHAPTER II

Standing in the railway carriage he constituted what a catholic taste might term a fine figure of a man – big and burly in his big overcoat, with plenty of colour in his dark, rather fleshy cheeks. His large nose was a little hooked; his thick lips were red and mobile; his dark eyes were intelligent but sly. The force of his personality was indubitable, he was clearly a man of energy and courage. But no cautious man would say it was an honest face; there was shiftiness to be read there, unscrupulousness, perhaps, and there was in no way any indication of intellect. And at the moment, as it had been when young Reddy had been so impressed, it was marked by every sign of violent bad temper. Nor was that bad temper soothed by the crowded state of the train, nor by the delays caused by the fog. Morris was stimulated to viciousness by the time he reached his station.

He elbowed his way out of the carriage, showing small regard for other people's toes and other people's ribs; he forced his way along the crawling queue which was passing through the ticket collector's gate, and then he crossed the main road and strode in a fury of bad-tempered haste up the tremendously steep hill to his house. It was an incline which would have tested the lungs of a man in good training when taken, as Morris did it, at five and a half miles an hour; Morris, a little too fat and quite out of condition, was gasping by the time he reached the top. That was nothing unusual, however. Morris was nearly always bad-tempered when he was going home, and he usually took that hill too fast in consequence.

At the top he was in the heart of the New Estate, as everyone about called it, despite the fact that it was already five years old. From the point of vantage at the top of the hill one could look round and down at hundreds of little houses of white stucco, red roofed, pitiful little places, terraces and crescents and squares; pitiful because they represented an attempt on the part of the County Council to build houses (which could be rented at prices not much too expensive for artisans, without imposing too great a burden on the rates) bearing the hall-marks of advanced civilization at a cost which utterly precluded them. They were semi-detached houses, each couple standing proudly in its own plot of land, but pathetic because if the houses had been big enough to be really habitable they would have filled their particular plots to overflowing. They had casement windows, which were quite pretty, save for the objection that to clean the outside of the hinged window one needed to climb up to it with a ladder from without, for to do it from within called for the services of someone with an arm nine feet long. The boilers were scientifically arranged so that the sitting-room fire heated the water, but by the time three people and their furniture were established in the house there was not an atom of space left in which to store the coal for the sitting-room fire.

Morris had meditated on these facts often enough before, and they had ceased actively to annoy him, but perhaps they contributed to the feeling of irritation which so often urged him up the hill faster than he ought to go. Tonight, perhaps, faced with the prospect of dismissal and starvation, he was not so much affected by them. He looked neither to the right nor to the left as he strode up the hill; he swung round at the very summit, for the corner house here, looking out across the Estate and the valley of the Mead clear to London, twelve miles away, was where he lived; had been his home for four years now.

A stride from the front door took him into the middle of the hall. He hung up his hat and coat and another stride took him into the sitting-room.

'Isn't that kid in bed yet?' was Morris's way of saying good evening to his wife. 'It's seven o'clock.'

'She's company for when you come back late like this,' retorted Mrs Morris. There never was a speech yet to which Mrs Morris had not a ready and devastating answer. That was one of the reasons of the quarrels between the two.

'Late?' demanded Morris. 'Call this late? Only luck I wasn't a dam' sight later. Kept at the office, fog on the line, it might have been ten by the time I got here. What've you got for my tea?'

'Nice bit of haddock,' said Mrs Morris, cautiously defensive. Food was a matter of so much interest to her husband that she had always to be ready to defend herself from his charges of feeding him insufficiently or unsuitably.

'Haddock? I'll have it now. No, put that kid to bed first.'

Molly, his daughter, was kneeling on a chair at the table scribbling on a piece of paper with a pencil. At any moment she might come and ask him to draw a horse for her, or a cat, or an engine. Molly had never learnt that her father had no desire whatever to draw horses for her.

There had once been a time, earlier in their married life, when symptoms of bad temper on her husband's part had had a subduing effect on his wife, spurring her to haste in obeying his wishes, causing her to walk on tiptoe about the room, to give him soft answers, to be in evident awe of him. But that had passed now. Mary Morris had learnt to 'stand up' for herself, as she put it, to counter commands with refusals, anger with defiance. Perhaps this had been partly because she did not love her husband so much now; certainly one cause was that she did not respect him so much now that she knew him better; but the main reason, perhaps, was that a quarrel did at least import some spice of variety into an otherwise drab life.

'No,' said Mary, 'let her stay up. She ain't doing any harm.'

'Seven o'clock is late enough for a kid her age. Bedtime, Molly.'

Molly looked round at him and then went on scribbling. As far back as her memory went there had been no need for instant obedience to one parent when the other was in opposition, and that was the usual state of affairs.

'Did you hear me, Molly?' thundered Morris.

This was a little more serious. Molly looked up to judge her mother's attitude before she went on scribbling again.

'God bless my soul!' said Morris, turning towards her.

10

But before he reached her her mother had darted in between them.

'Don't touch her,' she said, drawing up her skinny figure undismayed before his overbearing bulk. 'Don't you dare touch her. She's to go to bed when I say. I'm her mother.'

'Yes, you're her mother, you—'

The quarrel was well started now, on a familiar opening gambit. It developed on familiar lines; it ended half an hour later in a familiar stalemate, long after Molly had grown tired of scribbling. She had merely climbed down from her chair to play her usual obscure game of houses beneath the table, wherein the footstool represented not merely the entire household furniture, but visitors and tradesmen and, when necessary, the mistress of the house as well. The quarrel which raged over her head meant entirely nothing to her; it was as familiar a part of her world as was the hearthrug or the sideboard. The quarrel eddied round the sitting-room; it continued with long range indirect fire through the open door when Mrs Morris went into the kitchen and Morris flung himself into the armchair; it died away when Mrs Morris's dropping shots only called forth grunts and wordless noises of disgust from her husband; it seemed over when Mrs Morris reached below the table, brought Molly out, and started her up the stairs. Thereupon it promptly flared up again when Morris called some jeering remark after her. Mrs Morris could not possibly leave her husband the last word; she bounced down the stairs again and flung open the sitting-room door. Molly played on the stairs for five minutes before her mother returned and bustled her up to bed.

When Mrs Morris finally descended she found her husband sitting at the fireside silent and morose. She cooked his supper for him, put it on the table, and said, 'It's ready.' He heaved himself up to the table, ate and drank without a word, and went back in silence to his armchair. He was so subdued and depressed, in fact, that Mrs Morris credited herself with a victory unusually decisive in the recent argument, and felt a little pleased glow of achievement in consequence, which lasted her all the rest of the evening while she washed up and while she sat mending beside the fire.

Morris sat opposite her, chin in hand. He did not feel any urge that evening to listen to the wireless; he did not want to look again through the morning paper, nor even to put the advertisements in the latter through his usual critical examination. His sanguine temperament had led him to forget his troubles during his argument with his wife, but they returned with new force while she was upstairs putting Molly to bed. When, over his cup of coffee, he had described to Oldroyd so rhetorically the certainty and the unpleasantness of unemploy-

ment, he himself had not been so much affected by the prospect he was describing. Fear had been overlain by the irritation caused by the failure of his scheme for raising secret commissions. But fear came into its own now. Morris had no illusions regarding the fate of a city clerk dismissed with disgrace. His throat shut up a little, he felt a difficulty in breathing, as he realized in all its horror the imminence of dismissal, of tramping streets looking for work, of standing elbow to elbow with seedy out of works scanning the 'Situations Vacant' columns of the newspapers in the Free Library. He had tasted cold and hunger before, and he shrank with terror, even he, big burly Charlie Morris, from encountering them again. He felt suddenly positively sick with fear. Terror rippled down his skin even while he hunched himself closer to the fire's comfortable warmth. All men have their secret fear; Morris had discovered his only now that it was too late to save himself by mending his ways. He cursed himself for a fool even while he blanched with fear.

Soon he knew panic; he felt a positive impulse to get up from his chair and run away from these perils which were menacing him. If running away could have saved him he would have run all night through the darkened streets. Morris hitched his chair nearer to the fire instead.

The wailing of his two-year-old son upstairs brought an interval of distraction. John always cried for attention at ten o'clock; his parents had come to look upon it as the signal for bedtime. Mrs Morris put away her mending and hastened upstairs to him. Morris sat on by the fire for a moment, but habit came to his rescue. He got up from his chair, locked the back door, turned out the gas, passed into the hall, locked the front door, and made his way upstairs to bed.

This mechanical routine, and that following of undressing, had at least the effect of saving him from mad panic. And the chill of the sheets drove every thought from his mind for a time when he got into bed. So it was almost with pleasure that he encountered it – usually his thick body shrank from cold

12

welcome. He turned on his side; his wife came in and pottered about the room, the shadow of her skinny, half-naked figure fell across his face as she passed by him, but he did not open his eyes. Then the light went out and Mary climbed in beside him. The bed lost its chill; Mary turned on her side away from him and lay quiet. He was nearly asleep when the appalling realization of the future surged up again in his mind, and he was instantly broad awake again. Never before had worry kept him awake; the novelty of the experience redoubled its effect. Almost at once the bed seemed to become far too hot. Mary's body through her nightdress felt positively feverish to his touch as he came into contact with it when he turned in desperation to his other side. Now it was irritation as well as fear which was disturbing him. Why had he been such a cursed fool as to try that stunt for screwing money out of the Adelphi Studio? He might have known that little rat, Cooper, would go straight away and complain to Harrison. God, it was lucky that Campbell hadn't been there. He'd be on the street now in that case. There was still tomorrow to do something about it.

Desperation now had its effect of driving him into considering action. If only he could think of some way out of the mess! Pleading with Harrison wouldn't be any use. He knew Harrison. And Campbell, too. Campbell was a kindly old soul, but he would not forgive bribery. Everyone in the office knew that Campbell had refused a five-thousand-pound agreement with the Elsinore Cork people because they had wanted him to split the commission with them. Poor fool, Campbell. But Campbell was all right. He owned the business. No one could give *him* the sack, and he drew eight hundred a year out of it. Harrison got six quid a week – eight perhaps. Morris didn't know. He had wanted Harrison's job himself – might have got it, later on, if this blasted business hadn't happened. God, if only something would happen to Harrison – tomorrow. He'd be all right then. But what could happen to Harrison? He might be ill – but he would come back sooner or later. If he were to die – be run over in the Strand tomorrow morning – things would be different. Morris would get his billet then, most likely. Ah, but Harrison wouldn't be run over. Morris turned irritably over to his other side again as he realized how impossible was the thing he was longing for.

But perhaps it was at that moment that Morris took his first step on the path that lay before him. With Morris to desire

13

something urgently was to start planning how to bring it about. Turning this way and that in the fever-hot bed, his mind working faster and faster but more and more inconclusively, Morris did not notice how often the idea of Harrison's death came into his mind. A seed of rapid germination was being planted there.

Long after midnight his irritation and his anxiety turned to loneliness and self-pity. He put his hand out to Mary's thin body. She turned towards him, later, in response to his caresses, and, half asleep, returned with her thin lips the hot kisses Morris thrust upon her with his thick ones. Their arms went about each other in the darkness.


## CHAPTER III


The Universal Advertising Agency in James Street, Strand, would in the eyes of an unsympathetic person hardly have seemed important enough to rouse the emotions which surged so strongly in the breasts of the young men who composed three-quarters of its creative staff. It occupied a first-floor office. The reception room which one entered from the main door was furnished lavishly in good reception-room taste (for what that recommendation is worth), and the next room, which was Mr Campbell's, displayed painstakingly all the latest devices in office equipment which could conceivably find a place in a managing director's private room. Representatives of big businesses were ushered in here – men possibly with an advertising appropriation of a hundred thousand pounds to dispense – and it was necessary that they (who, ex officio, must know how a business should be run) should be suitably impressed with the efficiency of the Universal Advertising Agency.

But big business never penetrated beyond Mr Campbell's office. The next room, wherein were materialized the rosy visions which Mr Campbell poetically called up before the eyes of big business, was in striking contrast. There was not an armchair, nor a dictaphone, nor a desk of enamelled steel to be seen. Bare boards were all that composed the floor, blotched with ink – Mr Campbell's polished parquet and rugs stopped short at the threshold of the communicating door. Most of the space was occupied by half a dozen chipped and battered wooden tables, littered with papers and dog-eared files. Even these tables were allotted to the staff in a manner which displayed no decent attention to the rules of seniority. The centre one of the three under the long window was given over to the staff artist – the long-legged, weedy, lugubrious Mr Clarence – where he had the best of the light to assist him in his eternal task of lettering and rough sketching. As Mr Clarence said, his rough sketches might not perhaps be as good as Goya's finished work, but his lettering was better than any lettering which Sargent had ever exhibited; Goya and Sargent were people for whose work Mr Clarence had a very sincere admiration – a fact which constitutes a measure of how much Mr Clarence enjoyed his daily duties of lettering out 'Morish Marmalade' and 'Sleepwell Mattresses.'

On Mr Clarence's right sat Mr Oldroyd; on his left sat Mr Reddy. Behind them sat Mr Morris, but, as has been said, the decent rules of precedence were abruptly interrupted at this point by the fact that beside Mr Morris was the table of Shepherd, the office boy. Not that Shepherd was much at his table, because most of his time was occupied in journeys to studios, and printing offices, and newspaper offices, arriving everywhere, as Shepherd observed with fifteen-year-old pathos, half an hour late, without gaining his due credit for the fact that anyone not as efficient as Shepherd would have arrived half an hour later still.

Behind Mr Morris was the seat of power. Symbolically, perhaps, or perhaps so that he could better supervise the work of his juniors, Mr Harrison's chair and table were set on a low dais. It was here that the main decisions were reached; it was here that Mr Harrison held those conferences with representatives from commercial art studios which might result in the launching upon a surfeited world of some new mythical character, some Doctor Healthybody to advise the taking of Perfect Pills perhaps, or Sunray Toilet Soap Girl to declare that Ultraviolet Soap abolishes wrinkles. It was from this dais that Mr Harrison would step down with fitting solemnity to enter Mr Campbell's office to obtain his approval of the final idea.

On this particular morning Mr Harrison's frame of mind was peculiarly disturbed. There was no important work to

15

occupy him; a glance at the ruled and dated sheet pinned to his desk assured him that all the advertisements which the office were responsible for sending out that week were either despatched or were in process of final composition on the tables of Morris, or Oldroyd, or Reddy. There were no callers. Mr Campbell – 'Mac', as Mr Harrison thought of him – was in Glasgow and not due to return until tomorrow. Mr Harrison was free to make up his mind as to the action he would take on Mr Campbell's return. Mr Harrison set his lips and stared thoughtfully at the bent backs of his subordinates.

Reddy – his fair hair was illumined by the light from the window – was a good boy, although he had no brains. He would never have thought of the scheme which had been put into practice, which had resulted in the disappearance of the New Commercial Art Company's suggestions, in the consequent commissioning of the Adelphi Art Studios for a whole series of drawings, and in the payment of six pounds in secret commissions to the three young men before him. Reddy could be excused, perhaps, on the grounds that he had been led astray by the others.

Oldroyd, now. He was a good deal older, twenty-five at least, and he knew enough about the ways of the advertising world not to believe that the obtaining of secret commissions was an excusable frolic. But he had always been reliable up to the present. He had a nice eye for the lay-out of an advertisement, and he was sound on the subjects of sizes of type, and he was a careful proof reader. Mr Harrison realized that it would be a tedious business replacing Oldroyd if Oldroyd were dismissed. Lay-out men at three ten a week who could be relied upon to carry out routine work satisfactorily without supervision were hard to find; Mr Harrison flinched a little from the prospect of breaking a new-comer into the ways of the office and fitting him into the niche which Oldroyd filled so adequately. If Oldroyd showed himself properly contrite tomorrow, Mr Harrison might (although his mind remained open on the subject) put in that word with Mr Campbell which would save him from starvation and cold.

But it was quite a different matter as regards Morris. Mr Harrison bent his gaze almost with hatred on Morris's unresponsive back. He must have been the ringleader – that was clear to anyone who knew the three culprits. It was he who had devised the plan, and who had secured the co-operation of the

16

others. It was he who had filched in underhand fashion from Mr Harrison's authority, depriving him of a bit of that patronage which Mr Harrison dispensed with strict honesty but with a pleasant sense of his own importance.

Morris must go; there was no doubt about it. He had a wife, he had two children, and his savings, if he had any, must have been scraped out of a maximum income of four pounds ten a week. That did not affect the ethics of the case. Morris knew, when he concocted the plan, that he was exposing his wife and children to the chance of poverty and starvation. That was part of the stake he had risked; he had no right to grumble if he lost. Mr Harrison's conscience felt more comfortable as he reached this conclusion, because Mr Harrison was uneasily aware that he was glad that the chance had arisen of getting rid of Morris. The fellow was altogether too dangerous. More than once Mac had looked upon him with an approving eye, on the awkward occasions when a knotty point was under debate and a subordinate had been called in to the high councils of Mr Campbell and Mr Harrison. Morris then had had the impertinence to proffer a suggestion to Mr Campbell which Mr Harrison had already decided against, and Mr Harrison had had the mortification of seeing the suggestion accepted with delight, so that Mr Harrison had trembled for the security of his own job. Morris had too much sense of his own abilities. He could design advertisements with a 'punch'; he could form a sound estimate of the respective values of the different advertising media; he had plenty of energy and ambition (too much, thought Mr Harrison); and he was perfectly capable of coveting Mr Harrison's position.

Mr Harrison would never have dreamed of intriguing to get Morris out of the way. But now that the opportunity had presented itself Mr Harrison had no hesitation in seizing it. He hated the offence of which Morris was guilty – not once had Mr Harrison ever yielded to the thousands of similar temptations which came his way – he disliked the young chap personally, he distrusted him, and he was afraid of him. There was no mercy for Morris in Mr Harrison's mind. He would have dismissed Morris himself, bag and baggage, yesterday, had it not been for the fact that Mr Campbell had not delegated to him the power of dismissal.

Moreover, the internal debate within Mr Harrison's mind had somehow worked him into a bad temper. He set his thin lips and glowered at Morris's bent back with a voiceless rage. He disliked Morris much more now than he did half an hour ago. Perhaps his hatred made itself felt telepathically in the room. Oldroyd shifted uncomfortably in his chair. Reddy, with a despairing gesture, tore up the draft lay-out with which he had been experimenting. Clarence made use of the licence granted to an admitted artist to put his feet on his table and stretch himself. The only one that did not stir was Morris, who kept his thick shoulders bowed over his table, while ostensibly he occupied himself with reading the proofs of the new lubricating oil booklet, and while actually he gave loose rein to his racing thoughts.

The entrance of Maud, Mr Campbell's particular typist, with the letters she had been typing for Mr Harrison, provided a welcome break in the gloomy silence which enveloped the room. Mr Harrison could be jocular at any moment with one of the opposite sex.

'Well, Maud,' said Mr Harrison, 'this is the last day of your holiday.'

'My holiday, sir?' giggled Maud.

'Yes, when Mr Campbell comes back tomorrow you'll have to start in and do a spot of work, won't you?'

'Don't you think you give me enough to do, then?' asked Maud.

'Not as much as Mr Campbell does, now, do I? But today's the last day. No more packing up at half-past four when he comes back.'

'Half-past four? Oh, I never—'

'Oh, Maud, Maud!' said Mr Harrison. 'And it's Guy Fawkes' day today. I suppose it'll be half-past three this afternoon, because you want to get home and let your fireworks off.'

'I haven't got any,' said Maud. 'Too old for such things, Mr Harrison, don't you know. What about you, sir? Aren't you going to have any?'

'To tell the truth,' answered Mr Harrison, 'I *am* going to have some. Rockets and Catherine wheels and goodness knows what. *And* a bonfire.'

'Goodness!' said Maud.

'Oh, just for the kiddies,' said Mr Harrison off-handedly. 'They like it, you know. We've got the bonfire all piled up in the garden already. Fat lot of tea those kids'll let me eat when I get home tonight.'

Mr Harrison smoothed the wisps of hair over the bald top of his head and smiled benevolently. His conversation with Maud continued for several more minutes, but what he had already said was enough to make his fate certain.

Morris had been listening intently to every word he said, straining his attention so as not to miss a syllable; so intently and with such attention, in fact, that, absurd as it sounds, he had felt his ears move as he listened. Morris had the information he needed. He knew now that in the evening a state of affairs would arise when he could kill Mr Harrison. The trivial talk about fireworks and bonfires had given him that information. For Morris had been more than once about work to Mr Harrison's house on those occasions when bad colds kept Harrison from the office, and he knew the arrangement of Mr Harrison's house and garden.

If Morris had been asked about the matter by someone from Mars, let us say – someone at any rate of no influence at all in the world's affairs, and most certainly not in his own, someone to whom Morris could speak freely about his motives (which in practice would be quite inconceivable), he would have said in all sincerity that he had more right to kill Mr Harrison than Harrison had to have him dismissed. He would have said so, and believed it, and meant it, quite simply and literally. It was far more important to Morris that Morris should remain in employment than that Harrison should remain alive. If Harrison was bent upon dismissing Morris, and the only way to stop him was to kill him – then it was quite right to do so. Morris did not even pause to think this out. He leapt instantly to that conclusion. To his dying day he never saw any flaw in it.

That is why it is absurd to mention conscience in any discussion of this Morris affair. Morris was acting, it might be said, in accordance with the dictates of his conscience when he plotted Harrison's murder. It was right, in Morris's eyes, that he should not be sacked from the office. It was monstrously wrong if he should be, and that was the end of the argument. Morris had that disproportionate sense of the importance of his own well-being as compared with other people's which is one-half of the equipment of the deliberate murderer. The other factors Morris possessed as well – unfortunately for him, perhaps – the ingenuity to devise a plan, the imagination to attend to details and the resolution to carry it through.

The blood flowed hot under Morris's skin as he sat at his

table, with his back to Harrison, and worked out the possibilities of this opportunity which fate had presented to him. It was an exalted creative moment – Morris devising a murder was in the same lofty, superhuman state of mind as is a poet in the full current of composition. Thoughts poured through his brain in clear, rushing streams. This he could do, and that. This would guard against that possibility, and that would strengthen that weakness. Yes, and then— There seemed no limit to Morris's clear-sighted ingenuity at the moment, as he sat there, his left hand clenched, the fingers of his right tapping on the table, his head bowed in thought, and his heavy jaw setting harder and harder as his resolution became more and more fixed – as he realized more and more clearly that the thing was possible.

Clarence, the artist, stretched himself and rose from his chair.

'Don't you blokes *ever* feel hungry—' he inquired plaintively. 'One o'clock, and I'm off. O R P H. Anyone coming?'

The three looked at him, and with one accord they shook their heads and muttered refusals. They did not want to have Clarence with them while they continued their debate of the evening before about the matter which had dictated every thought since yesterday.

'All right,' said Clarence, reaching for his hat, 'be unsociable, if you want to. So long. I'll have that lettering done by about three, Mr Harrison.'

He lounged out of the room; his method of maintaining the dignity of Art was by displaying a careless lack of deference towards everyone, even towards Mr Harrison.

Mr Harrison rose as the door closed, and he reached for his hat, too.

'I'll get my lunch now, as well,' he announced. 'You three can do as you like as long as someone's here until I come back.'

He stepped down from the dais and walked towards the door. Perhaps if it had only been one yard to the door instead of five Mr Harrison would be alive now. As it was the two or three seconds which it took him to cross the room were too long for him to get through in silence; he was self-conscious under the gaze of three pairs of eyes, and with the knowledge that three people were waiting breathlessly to know his decision. And when Mr Harrison was self-conscious he talked. And on this occasion the only subject Mr Harrison could think of to talk about was the one which had occupied the minds of all four of them that morning.

'I haven't said anything to anyone as yet,' he announced, with his hand on the door-handle, 'about this business with the Adelphi Studio. We don't want the girls and Clarence talking until it has got to come out. I shall speak about it to Mr Campbell tomorrow morning, though.'

He looked round at them – Reddy with his frail figure and fair hair, Oldroyd bovine and stupid, Morris big and thickset and dangerous. It was that dangerous look about Morris which stung him into one last self-assertive remark.

'And if I were you,' he added, 'I should start thinking about hunting up another job. In the Colonies.'

Mr Harrison felt a vague satisfaction as he went down the stairs at having thus displayed his power, although he would perhaps hardly have considered it worth it had he foreseen that every word he had spoken was the equivalent of another nail in his coffin.

'That settles it,' said Oldroyd at the end of the pause that followed Harrison's departure. 'He means to get us the boot from Mac tomorrow all right.'

Oldroyd knew nothing of Mr Harrison's late decision to put in the deciding word on his behalf with Mr Campbell.

'Yes,' said Morris. He spoke with deliberation, and he looked steadily into the eyes first of Oldroyd and then of Reddy. He walked quietly over to the door of the room, pulled it open suddenly, and looked out. There was no one there – the office was empty. He shut it again and turned back. 'Yes, but – We've still got a chance. We've got till tomorrow.'

'What's the good of that?' grumbled Oldroyd. 'What are you going to do? Tell him you'll be a good boy if he'll let you off this time? He won't. You know what Harrison's like by now.'

'He'll tell Campbell, anyway, just to show off in front of him,' put in Reddy, with a perspicacity which surprised himself as much as the others.

'He will, ' said Morris still deliberately, 'unless we stop him.'

There was a hidden, grim meaning obviously underlying his words. The speech demanded a question.

'Stop him?' asked Reddy, almost in a whisper. He guessed somehow, at what Morris was hinting, which was more than Oldroyd did.

'Yes,' said Morris solemnly.

The superhuman exaltation had not left him yet. His mind was working with the rapidity and accuracy of a calculating machine. The glances he was darting at Oldroyd and at Reddy were reading their very thoughts. The force of his personality was overwhelming them steadily. Reddy was his man already; Oldroyd might soon follow.

'But how?' demanded Oldroyd; his tone of despairing contempt was not quite genuine.

'You've got a gun, haven't you?' asked Morris. 'A revolver?'

'That's so,' said Oldroyd, 'but—'

The weapon was a little plated affair of .22 calibre only, bought by Oldroyd two years ago, out of an unexpected bonus, for the usual motiveless motive which induces a very young man to buy a weapon.

'But—' said Oldroyd. 'Do you mean – murder, you fool?'

'That's what I mean,' said Morris.

'Bah!' said Oldroyd. 'Don't be a fool. I'm not going to have anything to do with it. You're mad.'

'No, I'm not,' said Morris. 'Do I look like it? Look at me.'

But Oldroyd was able to meet Morris's eyes with north-country stolidity. Morris saw his first plan for making Oldroyd an accomplice collapse into failure. It certainly had been a highfalutin idea to try and get Oldroyd to do the killing himself. But like lightning Morris was ready with his alternative scheme, and so quickly and easily that the others did not, could not, perceive the change.

'I'm not asking you to do anything,' said Morris. 'You needn't have anything to do with it at all. *I'll* do it all – with Reddy, here, to do a little bit for me. You won't be mixed up with it in any way. All I want is for you to lend me your gun.'

'What for?'

'You know what for as well as I do. But it won't make any difference to you – it won't incriminate you, I mean. It only makes me safer. I could go and buy a gun across the road there now. But if someone were to sell a revolver today and then read in the papers tomorrow that someone's been shot he *might* put two and two together. There's a bit of danger there.'

'Yes?'

'But if you lend me your gun. You can chuck it off Waterloo Bridge if you like afterwards. There'll be no danger there to you or to me.'

'But how are you going to do it?'

22

'To do it?'

'To do – what you were talking about.'

'Easy. Trust me for that. You know I'm not the sort of chap to make a mess of a simple job.'

'But—' said Oldroyd.

'God damn you and your "buts". That's the tenth time you've said "but" already,' burst out Morris. ' "But" this and "but" that – God bless my soul, man, d'you *want* to lose your job? You heard what Harrison said about the Colonies? You'd starve there the same as you would here, and you know it. It's November now. Five months of winter to go through. You've been out of work before, haven't you, you know what it's like? Nothing to eat and always damned cold. Sitting in a Free Library by the hot-water pipes until a porter turns you out. And it needn't happen if you just let me have that gun of yours for half an hour. You needn't know what I want it for. You'll be all right even if they catch me – which they won't.'

Oldroyd's solid north-country temperament made him a target worthy of all the arrows of Morris's impassioned rhetoric and artful pleading. It called for plenteous argument to convert him even to the contemplation of murder. Murder was a new idea to him, one which he had never considered before; he would have been slow to adopt it if its legality had been without question. Yet Morris could see that the objections he was raising were now more the result of obstinacy than of reason.

'They'll get you for certain,' said Oldroyd. 'Then they'll hang you.'

'If they do, as I said, it'll be my own look out. But they won't. D'you know how many murders there are each year where they don't find who did it? Dozens. And they won't get me. D'you think I'd be so keen on it if I thought there'd be any chance of that? Not likely. See here, Oldroyd. You know as well as I do that what they start to look for in these cases is *motive*. Who's got any motive for killing Harrison? They won't find anyone. Harrison said himself he hadn't told anyone about our business. I can work it all right and I can get away without being seen. Trust me for that, I tell you. What do the police do then? They come along. No one has the least idea who has done it. Well, say the police, who's likely to, or who wanted to? They ask his wife. They might come and ask Mac here. His wife doesn't know anyone who would. Nor does Mac. There is nothing more they can do. Shrug their shoulders and

23

say that probably someone made a mistake and got the wrong man. Or they might think it was done because of a woman – Mrs Harrison wouldn't know anything about that. And if they start looking along that line I don't know what they'll find, but they won't find me.'

'Oh, yes, it sounds all right,' said Oldroyd. He did not mean that; what he meant was it sounded all wrong, but that he could not define his objection accurately.

Morris took him literally for the purpose of his argument.

'Of course it's all right. For you it's absolutely all right. Look what you stand to win by it – you keep your job, and you might get Harrison's job as well. And what do you stand to lose by it? Nothing. Absolutely nothing. You're not fond of Harrison by any chance?'

'No, I'm not that,' replied Oldroyd reluctantly.

'Right,' said Morris.

It is doubtful whether Morris, on his own initiative, would have had the art to break off the argument there and allow his words to have their solvent effect on Oldroyd's inertia. Probably he would. He was in that superhuman mood of his, when his intellect was working at its very best. But, as it was, the decision was made for him. They heard a step in the corridor outside, and then women's voices. Instantly the three fell apart instinctively. Morris strode across to the door, pulled it open, and looked outside. There was no one in the corridor; the voices came from the room the other side.

'Maudie and Miss Knight have come back from lunch,' announced Morris to the others. 'What about it, you chaps? Coming now?'

The three of them strolled out of the room, but Morris's mind was still working at top speed. Before joining the others he peered into Mr Campbell's room. No one was there. He scuttled across and looked into the reception room. No one there. On their way out he looked into the typing room.

'Hullo, Maudie!' he said. 'Hullo, Miss Knight! What was it today? Baked beans on toast or a cup of tea and a bun?'

'Neither, Mr Knowall,' said Maudie. Morris's coarse good looks had rather an appeal for Maudie.

But that was all right. There were only those two in the room, and from the way in which they were taking off their hats and gloves they had clearly only just come in. There had been no one in the office listening to their conversation. No one

24

with his ear to the door to catch a few muttered words which might hang him later. It was most improbable, anyway, but— Morris's painful experience of being found out in his first misdemeanour had made him careful. From now on he was going to take no chances.

It was an odd luncheon party, in the teashop, the atmosphere stifling with heat and steam, and the ears deafened with the clatter of crockery. The three of them sat at their table eyeing each other. They were dallying with the idea of murder, although with so many listening ears around them no one dared to discuss the subject. They said nothing at all in consequence. They could only look at each other, apprehensively or inquiringly as the case might be, as they ate sausages and mashed potatoes and turned over in their minds the notion of shooting Mr Harrison.

## CHAPTER IV

The strain of the afternoon in the office was worse than in the morning. Even Harrison felt it, and came to regret more acutely than ever that Mr Campbell was out of London so that the business could not be settled out of hand. He welcomed the arrival of callers in consequence with a warmth that astonished them; even the men who came calling hopelessly soliciting business for quite impossible art studios. He rang up the printing office which the firm usually employed and wasted a large amount of the foreman's time talking about nothing at all important. Finally, when one of the two elegant young men who spent their time seeking new business for the Universal Advertising Agency came in bubbling over with a quite unjustifiable hope that a certain gigantic motor-car firm might be induced to entrust their advertising to the agency, he treated the matter as positively serious.

Glad of a chance to relieve the tension, he summoned Clarence and Morris to his table, and the four of them began solemnly to try to design advertisements which would induce the motor-car firm, at sight of them, to scrap their exceedingly efficient advertising staff and put their affairs in the hands of the Universal Advertising Agency. Clarence stood at one shoulder, and Morris stood at the other, while the elegant young man hopped about in front in bewildered pleasure at having been taken seriously in this fashion. Slogans were debated: 'Nebuchadnezzar Cars won't eat grass, but they consume very little petrol.' Mr Harrison even considered verse:

> *'Whatever the make or type of your car,*
> *You'd do better still with a Nebuchadnezzar.'*

Twice Clarence was sent away to rough out a plan which had momentarily caught Mr Harrison's fancy, and each time he was called back because Mr Harrison had suddenly thought of a better plan still. Morris stood at his shoulder, shifting his weight from one foot and then from the other.

'Nebuchadnezzars Are – as – Lively,' said Mr Harrison, speaking in Large Type, 'when your Foot is on the Brake – as Other Cars are – when you step on the – Accelerator. What do you think about that, Morris?'

Yesterday, before he knew that he was going to be dismissed, Morris would have played for safety. He would have accorded moderate praise to the suggestion – praise because it never pays to sneer at one's superior's ideas, yet moderate because Mr Harrison probably would change his mind about it later – and because Mr Campbell would veto the idea for certain. But today, with safety out of reach, and a very bad night behind him, and his head full of another idea altogether, Morris was incapable of displaying tact. He looked at Mr Harrison's vague outlines. He turned over in his mind Mr Harrison's astonishing headlines. Then he gave a considered judgement.

'I think,' said Morris slowly, 'I think it's all—'

What Morris said it was cannot be written here. He used vulgar bad language with astonishing point and vigour. It called forth a grin on Clarence's face; it made Oldroyd and Reddy mistrust their hearing. All the same, it was an excellent criticism of Mr Harrison's little notion. But it made Mr Harrison compress his lips and flush bright pink.

The etiquette of bad language in advertising offices is quite elastic. A senior can use it before a junior without hesitation. A junior, provided he is sufficiently deferential, can use it before a senior on subjects indifferent to both. But no junior can ever, ever, ever say the words Morris employed about a senior's

26

own special suggestion. Yet, after all, finished advertisements are usually the product of combined effort, and even destructive criticism, by the tradition of the profession, should be welcomed. Anyone can give an adverse criticism of an advertisement quite safely, because he has only to pose as a half-witted member of the half-witted general public for whom the designer intends the advertisement. If he does not like it, then a section at least of the public will not like it either, and the originator ought to be glad to hear about that before spending further time over it.

It was this convention which tied Mr Harrison's hands. He swallowed the insolence with an effort.

'Umph,' said Mr Harrison, struggling with his feelings. 'We'd better try some other line, then. What about—'

His new suggestion was hardly more effective, and Mr Harrison knew it. What was particularly annoying to Mr Harrison was the feeling that he had only started this discussion in order to bring about a more amicable atmosphere in the office, and this was a poor return for his kindly efforts. And Morris displayed a lamentable lack of tact again. After his first outburst he left off being rude, but he was not encouraging. He showed up the weakness of Mr Harrison's idea in a few brief sentences. He did it again later, tired of fidgeting about first on one foot and then on the other while Mr Harrison prosed on about impossibilities. His blunt, pigheaded criticisms eventually drove Mr Harrison distracted.

'Good Lord lumme,' exploded Mr Harrison, slapping down the papers on the table, 'I might as well be trying to make up ads with a – a mule! And what in hell are you laughing at, Reddy? I'm sick to death of the whole pack of you. Thank God that—' he checked himself. Clarence and the other young fellow were in the room, and it was undesirable that they should know of the scandal in the office. But the words he had intended to finish the sentence were plain enough to anyone in the secret.

'What's the time?' went on Harrison, changing the subject. 'Five o'clock? I'm going out to get a cup of tea. Send Shepherd round to Spott's for those new pulls as soon as he comes back. And have those roughs for the Scottish Series ready for me when I come back.'

He went out, and the three guilty ones looked at each other. Even Oldroyd felt a stirring of hero worship for this vigorous

27

young man who had said to Harrison exactly what Oldroyd had wanted to say on several occasions. As for Reddy, he blinked at Morris, standing flushed and magnificent on the dais, as he would have blinked at the sun in splendour. The elegant young man, annoyed at this sudden neglect of his fine idea, picked up his hat and his gloves and his cane and lounged out again after Mr Harrison. Clarence, whistling dolefully, threw himself into his adjustable chair and filled his brush with his Indian ink. Morris beckoned Reddy across to him where he still stood at Harrison's table, and Reddy came, docile.

'I want you tonight,' Reddy,' said Morris in a low voice. Reddy nodded. 'I want you and your motor-bike. That's running all right, I hope?'

'Yes,' said Reddy.

'Good! Meet me down by Meadwell Station. Can't say what time – depends on when we get away from here. Go straight home, get your bike out, and come along to pick me up. We'll be going to Oldroyd's *first*.'

Reddy merely nodded again. No saving sense of reality came to help him. He was Morris's man, first and last, at present. Murder was a queer, impossible happening. He could picture no possible horror resulting from their expedition this evening. Perhaps if he had been asked he would have said that he expected nothing to happen. Any dreadful vague event in the future was of small importance compared with the certainty of losing Morris's friendship on the spot by hesitation now. Morris looked at him with a smile and led him back across the room, arm in arm. It is impossible to say how Morris had acquired this happy certainty of the force of his own personality. But, with a mind wrought up to fever pitch, he was full of certainty and efficiency. There were two things which had brought him to this high level – extreme danger and the need for intrigue. Between them they had changed Morris from a rather slack lay-about clerk into a man of extreme elasticity of thought and vigour of resolution.

He passed behind Clarence, who was bent over his lettering, and leaned over Oldroyd's shoulder as he stared rather blankly at the advertisement pasted on a sheet of foolscap which he had to redesign.

'I will be coming round to your place this evening,' said Morris in his ear. 'I won't be stopping long. Only just call for something.'

Oldroyd turned his head and stared at him over his shoulder. Their eyes met at a range of a foot, Oldroyd's nondescript hazel eyes staring into Morris's lustrous brown ones. They might have posed at that moment, the two of them, for a mediaeval picture – Satan muttering temptation into the ear of some surprised artisan.

'Do you understand?' asked Morris. He mouthed the words rather than said them.

Oldroyd nodded. He was fascinated too. And to him, as to Reddy, the whole business seemed too fantastic to be believable. Also, even though this feeling of improbability was not quite so numbing as in Reddy's case, he was supported by the comfortable feeling that he, anyway, would not be involved. His mind had not the penetrative power to see any flaws in Morris's arguments at present, and Morris had spoken plausibly enough. By the time Morris turned that magnetic stare away from him and went back to his place Oldroyd's slow decision had been formed to join Morris in the plan. He might have changed his mind once more had he been given twenty-four hours to think it over. But as it was he had no more than two – half an hour before Harrison returned and gave them leave to go, and an hour and a half spent in travelling home and waiting for Morris to arrive.

## CHAPTER V

Young Reddy had no difficulty in going out again on his motor-bicycle as soon as he reached home.

'It's important, Mother,' he said in reply to her very slight expostulation, and she smiled indulgently and let him go. 'Boys will be boys,' was one of the expressions most frequently on her lips, and she could even smile bravely at the thought that it must be a girl whom he was going to see so 'importantly'.

Twenty minutes by cross-roads took him from his own suburb to Morris's, and there, outside the station, Morris was standing, in his heavy overcoat with his collar up to his ears. Reddy drew up at the kerb, and Morris threw his leg over the back wheel and sat himself on the pillion without the need for shutting off the engine. Reddy put in the clutch again and they were off.

'Stop at the corner this side of Oldroyd's place,' said Morris in Reddy's ear as they whirled away through the darkness.

Once more they had a cross-country route but a brief one this time. With Charing Cross Station so near to their office, nearly all the staff of the Universal Advertising Agency lived in the limited area served by the suburban line running south-eastwards from there.

'Wait for me here,' said Morris as they drew up in the dark street, and he left Reddy there still astride of his saddle while he hurried off round the corner.

Oldroyd lived in lodgings, the kind of lodgings a young man without a relation in the world and with a salary of three pounds ten a week might be expected to inhabit. The little maid, who knew Morris by sight, admitted him at once and sent him up the stairs to Oldroyd's room. Oldroyd was stand-ing at the window looking out into the night; he had not seen Morris's arrival at the gate, and he turned sharply at his en-trance.

'I haven't got a lot of time to spare,' said Morris. 'Let's have the thing, quick.'

Oldroyd hesitated, turned towards the drawer in which lay the revolver, turned back again. His hands were writhing with his anxiety.

'Oh, buck up, man!' said Morris, but Oldroyd still hesitated. He could neither resist Morris nor abet him.

'Oh, well,' said Morris, and he walked over to the drawer. The key was in the lock – Oldroyd had handled the fascinating thing and then had put it back again already that evening. Morris pulled open the drawer and took out the revolver. It was a pretty little toy; it held no menace in its elegant form. Morris looked to it carefully. He took out the cartridges, squinted down the barrel, saw that the mechanism was in good order.

'Only five cartridges?' he asked.

Oldroyd wetted his lips; it was only at the second attempt he was able to speak.

'They're all I've got,' he said hoarsely.

'Five'll be enough,' said Morris, and he replaced the cart-ridges with extreme care.

Then he slipped the weapon into his big overcoat pocket.

'Goodbye,' said Morris, and he turned towards the door.

It was only when the door was in the act of closing behind him that Oldroyd was able to speak again, and then he could only croak out 'Morris!' in his strangely hoarse voice. A little laugh came to him through the door, and he heard Morris's feet go clattering down the stairs. Next moment the door banged and it was too late. Oldroyd fell into a chair with his head in his hands. Morris walked back to where Reddy awaited him, with a lighthearted step. He felt no fear; it might be said with truth that he felt no excitement. The exaltation of spirit which possessed him was something he had never known before; it was rather a delicious feeling. It was splendid to find oneself facing a considerable danger without fear, holding all the threads of a tangled skein without confusion, keeping track of quite a large number of different facts and possibilities without difficulty. Over his head, as he came to the waiting Reddy, a rocket rose and burst into red and green stars. The earliest men to leave their city offices were home now, and had started to let off fireworks for the amusement of their children. Other rockets were to be seen in different quarters of the sky, here, there, and everywhere. The reports of all sorts of little explosions came to his ears as he stood by the motor-bicycle. Guy Fawkes' night was a popular holiday. He turned to Reddy.

'You ever been to Harrison's place?' he asked.

Reddy shook his head.

'It's over that way. Between here and Eltham. Go up the road here, cross the arterial road, and bear over to the right when I tell you.'

Reddy thrust at his kick-starter, and Morris perched himself anew on the pillion. They roared through the quiet suburban streets, crossed the arterial road, brilliant with the headlights of the thousand cars, and plunged once more into the new residential quarters the other side.

'Next on the right,' called Morris into Reddy's ear. 'Now second on the left. Slow here, there's a bit of traffic. Now second on the right, and stop at the corner.'

The noise of the engine dwindled and then stopped abruptly.

'Leave the bike here,' said Morris. Even he could not help whispering in the excitement of the moment.

'Up this way; come along,' continued Morris. With a hand on Reddy's arm he led up a narrow pathway between two houses. As they walked Morris noticed with satisfaction that it

31

was freezing hard; there was no chance of their leaving foot-prints. Just one more circumstance noted by Morris's amazing mind.

'Along here,' whispered Morris. They were walking now along a footpath which ran between the gardens of two parallel rows of houses.

'Now wait there,' said Morris. He thrust Reddy back against the hedge and took two or three steps forward and to the oppo-site side of the footpath. He halted and peered forward. Not satisfied with the position, he moved along the hedge until he came to a point where it was not so high, and where he had a full view of Mr Harrison's back garden. With his hat down to his eyes and his overcoat collar up to his nose, he stared for·ward, every line of his attitude indicating the tenseness of his mind and his muscles. One hand was in his right-hand side overcoat pocket.

Five yards before him there smouldered a bonfire. At the further end of the garden, nearer the house, there could be dimly made out a little group of people – adults and children. Morris could hear them laughing; fireworks were flickering and popping. All round him, in the hundreds of other suburban gardens, there was to be seen the glow of bonfires; fireworks were exploding with noises varying between the loud bangs of maroons and the smaller, flatter report of squibs. Morris waited grimly. He had not to wait for long. The little group at the far end of the garden broke up; two or three of its mem-bers came running up to the bonfire. Harrison was one of them. Two children were with him. He seized a pole and stirred the bonfire. An avalanche of sparks shot upwards; a mass of ruddy flames illumined Mr Harrison as he stirred the fire.

Morris's pistol was out now; he was braced and ready. Yet even then he waited a moment longer for a clear shot, until Mr Harrison showed up distinctly beside the fire, and until the children were out of the way. Then Morris pointed the pistol and pressed the trigger. Morris was a good shot with that .22-calibre revolver – much Sunday target practice out on the Downs with Oldroyd had made him so. And he would never have planned the attempt in this way if he had not had con-fidence in this way. At the first shot Mr Harrison staggered and put his hand to his breast. At the second he pitched forward on to his face into the fire. His bald head shone in the red glow; Morris saw the long wisp of hair which was trained over the bald patch from the side hanging sideways before it burnt away. But Mr Harrison writhed as he lay upon the fire and Morris, who knew that two shots from a .22-calibre revolver cannot be relied upon to kill a man, fired rapidly his three last cartridges into Mr Harrison's heaving back. Then he turned away, thrusting the pistol back into his pocket.

He seized Reddy's arm and began to walk him back the way they had come. Reddy was half silly with newly realized horror.

'Not too fast, blast you,' growled Morris. 'We don't want to attract people's notice.'

His thick muscular hand held Reddy's arm with a reassuring grip.

'Down here again,' said Morris, and a moment later they were back at the motor-bicycle.

'Now back to Oldroyd's,' said Morris.

Reddy was hardly conscious of doing anything by now; it was Morris who jerked up the stand into position and half thrust Reddy into the saddle. Reddy found his hands on the handlebars; half dazed still, he automatically adjusted air and throttle and thrust at the kick-starter. The engine was still hot and started instantly. A moment later they were away. They had hardly taken five minutes over the whole business; no one had seen them arrive, and no one had seen them go.

Morris, watching grimly over Reddy's half-drunken steering, could afford to feel pleased with himself. On that night of all nights no one would possibly have paid any particular attention to the sound of five pistol shots from a small calibre weapon. They had attracted no notice, just as Morris had expected. Not even now, five minutes after they had killed Harrison, did anyone know that Harrison had been murdered. Even Harrison's wife, bending distractedly over the body which she had dragged from the fire, was not aware of it. She had not seen the five tongues of flame which had shot from the hedge. Not until ten minutes later, after neighbours had carried Harrison into the house and the doctor had arrived was the discovery made. And by that time Morris and Reddy were three miles away, in Oldroyd's room.

Oldroyd started with surprise as they entered unceremoniously – Morris had merely turned the handle of the street door and led Reddy straight up the stairs of the room.

'Well?' said Oldroyd. 'What—'

33

He saw the elation in Morris's face. He looked at the clock; Morris had hardly been away a quarter of an hour. At first he thought with relief that nothing serious had happened. But a further glance told him that something must have happened to account for the look of brutal triumph in Morris's face. Then he saw Reddy's white cheeks and somnambulist expression, and the look of relief in his own face faded dramatically.

Morris peeped suddenly out of the door again. Reassured, he strolled into the centre of the room.

'All finished,' he said. 'Most satisfactory. And here's your little toy back again.'

With that he tossed the revolver on to the bed, where Oldroyd stared at it in fascinated horror.

'I don't want the thing. Take it away yourself, can't you?'

Morris laughed. He laughed at Oldroyd's evident terror. He laughed at white-faced little Reddy, still standing huddled in the corner. Most of all he laughed for joy at his own splendid success. The others looked at him as he rocked with mirth in Oldroyd's armchair. They had never felt less like laughing in their lives. But Morris's laughter died away in time, and his features set in an expression of brutal resolution – the same expression, in fact, as had characterized his face in the darkness at the moment of pulling the trigger.

'Look here, you blokes,' he said, 'there's no use pulling long faces over this business. You've got to brace up, and quick, too. I can't have you looking like this. The thing's done and we've got to make the most of it. We're as right as rain if we only keep our heads – it couldn't be better. But one slip even now, one little suspicious action, and we're all for it. All.'

He was speaking quietly, lest his voice should be heard beyond the room, but for all that he managed to throw a world of horrible menace into the last monosyllable. Oldroyd stared at him blankly.

'All?' he said.

'Yes!' snapped Morris. 'You're in it as much as me, both of you. Suppose anything comes out and I'm pinched? Where did I get the gun? From you. Where did I come just before it happened. Here. Where did we come as soon as it was finished? Here. Who took me to the place on his motor-bike and brought me back again? Reddy did. Who profits just as much as I do by it? You both do. And that's what I'll say if I get into trouble. I'll shout it at the top of my voice all day long. By God, I'll have 'em thinking before the end that I was led astray, and that you were the ringleader of the business – or this poor fool here.'

But Oldroyd was in as pitiable a state as Reddy now. His jaw had dropped and his eyes were wide and blank with dismay. Not until now had he realized how damning was the evidence of his complicity.

'It's not only the man who pulls the trigger who is guilty, you know,' went on Morris remorselessly, telling Oldroyd no more than he knew already; 'everybody who aids in any way before or after is just as guilty. People have been hanged quite lately for much less than *lending a weapon*, Oldroyd, or taking the killer to the place and back, Reddy. We've got to hang together this time, one way or another.'

Morris thought this last remark was an excellent joke, and could not help laughing at it all over again.

'You'll never convince anyone this wasn't a conspiracy,' he continued. 'And, of course, that's just what it was. Why, you poor blighters, you never used your brains. Now that Harrison's dead there are only two people on earth who know I had any motive for killing him. And they're you two. D'you think I'd have been such a fool as to risk my neck without taking precautions? I *had* to get you incriminated as well. And that's what I've done properly, haven't I?'

Morris was a 'bad winner', and as objectionable in consequence after a successful murder as he would have been after a lucky rubber of bridge. The jeering triumph in his tone was maddening to the wretched young men he was addressing. There was no advantage, in his eyes, left in maintaining the pretence of leadership and friendliness, and there was sweet balm to his vanity in displaying himself as the successful deceiver, and them as the pitiful dupes. He revelled in it, delighting in their consternation as proof positive of the triumph of his double dealing.

'You devil!' said Oldroyd with dull hatred. 'You beast!'

Reddy had sat down by now. He was still mazed and dizzy. A glance at him displayed to Morris the new danger – not of any voluntary admission on the part of Oldroyd, but of an involuntary one by Reddy. He met it with all his new readiness and eloquence.

'See here,' he said, and his voice had lost its jeering tone, 'I didn't mean all I said just now. It wasn't till afterwards – really

35

it wasn't – that I realized how much you two were dragged into it. Reddy, old man, the thing's done now. Remember that. It's done and can't be undone. We can't do Harrison any good now. We can't bring him back to life again. And, remember, it's *hanging* for us if we're found out – for Oldroyd as well as you and me. You don't want to let Oldroyd down, do you, old man? Pull yourself together now, come on, sonny.'

It was extraordinary what influence he still had over the boy. Reddy seemed to come back to life as he spoke to him. It had been nervous excitement rather than horror which had affected him at first; and later the revelation of Morris's cynical duplicity had been more shocking than Harrison's murder – at present. Morris was not a promising idol to set up for hero worship, but Reddy had done so, and he was still glad to replace him on his pedestal.

'That's better,' said Morris slowly. 'Now, look here, you chaps. We've still got a bit of business to arrange for tomorrow. Not much, but something, I expect the police will be up at the office tomorrow, asking questions. They'll be just as puzzled as Mac will be by this affair. They won't ask *us* much. They may not even ask us anything. You remember what I said this morning? They'll be looking for a motive. They won't think that any of us would have sufficient motive for – murder.'

(Even Morris could not utter that word without a trace of hesitation.)

'That's so,' agreed Oldroyd bitterly. But Morris was watching Reddy's face. It was showing a little more vitality and colour.

'All we've got to do is be natural. *Natural*. We don't know of any enemies he could have. Can't think of anyone. We can be surprised, sorry, worried, anything you like, as long as we're *natural*. Got that, *Reddy*, old man?'

Reddy agreed. It was the first word he had spoken since before the killing.

'That's all right then. And the other thing is – I don't expect they'll ask us, but we had better be ready for everything – if they want to know what we were doing this evening, we have been together the whole time. I came here first; we were expecting Reddy, and when I went out to get a paper and some cigarettes I met him and brought him in with me. That's all. We're as safe as houses. Why, we weren't gone twenty minutes altogether, and no one here could give anything like exact times

36

of our comings and goings. Oh, my goodness, we couldn't be safer!'

'And what about *this*?' said Oldroyd, indicating the revolver gleaming on the bed. He hated having to ask Morris anything, but he would have hated more having to pick up the deadly thing.

'Oh, I'll get rid of it, then. I suppose we'd better. Someone *might* come across it, and I've read in some book or other that they can prove by marks on the bullets which pistol they've been fired from. I'll go down on the Embankment and drop it into the river when I find a quiet place.'

Morris took the pistol again and thrust it into his overcoat pocket. Then he looked at his watch.

Eight o'clock. We've been talking over an hour! I'll be late home tonight, seeing I've got to go back to town with this thing. And I haven't had anything to eat since lunch. Anything more to settle? I don't think there is.'

The other two were silent as ever. They were both of them a little impressed, all the same, by this man of steady nerves who could talk so casually about eating. Oldroyd had left his supper almost untasted before Morris's first arrival, and Reddy had not thought of food since lunch-time.

'All right. I'm pushing off now. See you tomorrow; and don't forget what I said. You two had better go to the pictures or something; you can't sit there looking at each other all the evening. Yes, you'd certainly better. Come on. Get your coat on, Oldroyd. I'll come with you as far as the cinema.'

In the empty train which roared back to town with Morris on board Morris was at last able to indulge in justifiable exaltation; and walking along the dark Embankment from Charing Cross Station he grew, with the pleasant exercise of fast walking, almost intoxicated with the sense of achievement. As the novelist feels when he writes the last few lines of what he knows to be a masterpiece, and as the artist feels when, tired but happy, he sits down at last to contemplate his finished picture, so felt Morris as he strode along the Embankment. The sense of perfect achievement, so perfect that neither mortal man nor artistic conscience can suggest anything which could be an improvement, is attained by few indeed. Morris knew it then in all its flooding pride.

He had nearly reached Blackfriars before he found the place he sought. Not a soul within a hundred yards of him. He leaned his elbows on the parapet and looked down into the dark water. Then he dropped the weapon in. Twenty feet of water and ten feet of mud made a safe enough hiding place for a very dangerous piece of evidence. Then he turned back to Charing Cross Station again, to his home and his wife and his children.

'Late *again*?' said his wife when he came into the sitting-room.

But this time there was no hot reply from him. In fact, there was no reply at all; he merely lurched to the fireside and sat down. Although he was still glowing with triumph the reaction was beginning to have its way. He knew now that odd pain in the pit of the stomach and the unpleasant sensation of nausea combined with appetiteless hunger which every creative artist comes to know after a long spell of good work. His wife, noticing his flushed cheeks and his uncertain step, came instantly and naturally to the conclusion that he had been drinking, and was surprised. Morris had been a model husband in that respect; he had not come home the worse for drink more than three times in five years of married life. Mrs Morris thought none the worse of her husband in consequence of her suspicion; it did not happen often enough to be worrying, and when it did it constituted a pleasant break in the monotony of a life devoted to children, mending and supper-getting.

' 'Ve you been drinking?' she demanded.

'No,' said Morris; but, of course, he would have said the same whether he had been drinking or not.

Mrs Morris came near enough to smell his breath. Curious, but there was no trace of it there.

'Umph,' said Mrs Morris; then: 'D'you want any supper?'

'Yes,' said Morris.

But when it was put before him he found he could not eat more than a mouthful. He drank two cups of tea thirstily and then pushed his chair from the table.

'Don't you want to eat it after all?' asked his wife, thoroughly puzzled by this time. If the occasions when her husband was drunk had been rare, the occasions when he was not hungry had been rarer still.

Morris went back to his fireside chair, but he had not sat there more than five minutes before he was wearily on his feet again. He did not feel as though he could sit still any longer. He wandered round the room, his wife watching him, astonished.

'Oh, I'm going to bed,' said Morris. 'Good night.'

But he was not asleep when his wife came up, nor until long after. His mind was continuing its racing activity long after his body had begun to cry for mercy. No wonder, for his mind was still intoxicated with the pride of achievement.

And if the iconoclast would point out that Morris had not achieved anything very remarkable, that his way had been smoothed for him at every turn, the reply is that that does not make his success less remarkable. The perfect murder can only be achieved not merely when circumstances are highly favourable, but when the murderer is clever enough to make the most of circumstances and resolute enough to wring every possible advantage from them. The fact that it had been Guy Fawkes' Day had made the sound of his revolver unremarkable, and had brought Mr Harrison comfortably into range. But a less resolute murderer would have hesitated even then; might have dilly-dallied for the very few hours which would have enabled the golden opportunity to slip out of reach. And it called for quite a clever murderer's brain to work out, first, that the number of people who would know of his motive was very small indeed, and, second, how to incriminate those people so that they had the best of all reasons – the only reliable reason, in fact – not to disclose their knowledge. And what art and skill Morris had displayed in inducing them into joining him! It had been a brilliant, an unrivalled piece of work. There are very, very few known murderers who can lay claim to a rank nearly as high as Morris's. Compared with him Crippen was a pusillanimous fool and Armstrong a thoughtless scatterbrain. But this comparative praise says little enough for Morris, after all. He was only the best of a very poor lot.

## CHAPTER VI

Morris arrived early at the office next morning. The blind relief in his own good fortune which obsessed him left him with no lurking fears; he had no desire to postpone the interviews which he was certain were inevitable, and, moreover, Mr Campbell was the soul of punctuality and liked to see his staff arriving five minutes before time. But, early as he was, Maudie was there before him, and as he entered she looked out into the corridor from the typewriting room with its label, 'Inquiries'.

'Oh, it's you, Mr Morris,' she said. 'Something awful's happened.'

'Somebody pinched the safe?' asked Morris. It was surprising how cool and self-assured he was.

'Oh, no. Something *awful*. Mr Harrison was killed last night. There's a detective here now, and he told me. He's in the reception room now.'

'Good God!' said Morris. 'What was it? Accident or something?'

'I don't know. I don't think so. He wouldn't tell me. I think it was – worse than that.'

'What do you mean?'

'Oh, I don't know. Isn't it awful! To think he was here talking to me only yesterday!'

Maudie was one of those people who are utterly unnerved at hearing of the sudden death of the most distant acquaintance. Morris felt a pitying contempt for her as she stood there wringing her hands.

'Well, what had I better do about it?' asked Morris. 'Shall I go in and see him?'

'I don't know. It was Mr Campbell he asked for, and I said he'd be here in a minute. Oh, thank God, here he is!'

Mr Campbell was received by Maudie in the same fashion and in almost the same words as Morris was. Meanwhile the detective, standing just inside the reception-room door not a yard away, made a mental note that this fellow, Morris, seemed to be all right.

Mr Campbell received the news with a gravity even more marked than usual. Rubbing his chin thoughtfully, he turned into the reception room; outside Maudie and Morris heard their voices, of a normal pitch at first, die away into more confidential tones. Then evidently they went through into Mr Campbell's room. The other typist arrived, and then Shepherd the office boy, and after them Clarence the artist and the two young men who acted as travellers. All of them were drawn into a whispering, startled group outside the typing room. Last of all came Oldroyd and Reddy, together, and late, as Morris had expected. He looked keenly at them as they came in. Both of them, to anyone in the secret, showed signs of anxiety and

40

sleeplessness. Reddy even faltered a little in his steps as he caught sight of the agitated group. But they would pass muster, thought Morris. And little enough strain was imposed upon their powers of acting, because hardly had they arrived when the buzzer sounded in the typists' room, and Maudie, hurrying into Mr Campbell's office, emerged directly, and everyone stopped to hear what she had to say.

'We're to stop this talking,' said Maudie, 'and get on with our work as usual. How can I get on with my work? Mr Campbell can't see his mail yet. Oh, and he wants you to go in to him, Mr Morris.'

'Right ho,' said Morris. He stopped to take off his hat and coat, hung them up in the composing room, and stepped casually across to Mr Campbell's door. The others eyed him half curiously, almost enviously, before they dispersed. Morris knocked and entered.

No one could have mistaken the moustached man sitting beside Mr Campbell's desk to be other than the police officer he was.

'Good morning, Morris,' said Mr Campbell. 'Have you heard about this shocking affair?'

'Yes, sir. Miss Woods told me about it when I came in.'

'You didn't see anything in the papers about it this morning?' asked the police officer casually.

'No. I hardly looked at the paper this morning. Mr Marshall – that's one of our travellers – had seen a bit about it. But not very much.'

'No, not very much, I expect,' said the police officer, pulling his moustache.

'What this gentleman wants to know,' said Mr Campbell, 'is whether you can think of anything likely to throw any light on the matter. I must confess I am quite at a loss myself.'

'So am I,' said Morris.

'Do you know of anyone who had reason to dislike this man Harrison?' asked the police officer. 'Has anyone uttered threats against him to your knowledge?'

'I've been trying to think of something like that,' said Morris. 'But I can't think of anything. Mr Harrison got on well with everyone.'

Morris appeared to think deeply.

'No, he didn't have a single enemy as far as I know,' he announced at length.

'Was there anything odd about his behaviour yesterday?'

'Um. Nothing special. He seemed a bit short-tempered last night, but nothing to speak of.'

'Short-tempered about what?'

'Oh,' said the police officer, clutching at straws, 'he was angry with you yesterday, was he?'

Morris saw the danger, and met it with all his bold self-confidence.

'No, not specially. He was a bit irritated about work.'

'This kind of work,' put in Mr Campbell, 'is a little bad for one's nerves at times.'

The police officer saw this faint hint of a motive disappear.

'Did he ever speak of any danger threatening him?' he asked, going off on a new tack. 'Did he ever seem anxious or worried without any particular reason?'

'No,' said Morris decidedly. 'He didn't even worry about money very much.'

The police officer pulled at his moustache as though he wanted it to come out by the roots.

'Well, now, Mr – er – Morris,' he said at length, 'was he ever involved in any trouble with a woman? Did you ever hear of any entanglement in that way?'

'No,' said Morris, treating the delicate subject with a graceful tact. 'No, I never heard of anything in that way. Of course it wouldn't be likely that I would. But he didn't seem that kind of man at all, did he, Mr Campbell?'

Mr Campbell agreed. He had answered the same question himself in the same fashion only five minutes ago.

'And the other men working with you, went on the police officer, 'were they all on good terms with Mr Harrison?'

'Yes, quite,' said Morris definitely.

Then suddenly the police officer launched the question he had been saving up in reserve – his Old Guard of a question.

'What were you doing yesterday evening, Mr Morris?' he demanded abruptly.

'Me? I went round to Oldroyd's place when I left here. I stayed there a bit – until eight, I think, or a bit later. Reddy was there, too. Then Reddy and Oldroyd went to the pictures, and I went home.'

'Reddy?' asked the police officer. 'Oldroyd?'

'They are the other two men working with Mr Morris under Mr Harrison,' explained Mr Campbell.

'Oh, so you spent part of the evening together, did you, Mr Morris? I wonder if you would mind telling me why?'

Morris allowed a flash of righteous indignation to escape from his eyes at this veiled hint. He caught Mr Campbell's eye, and Mr Campbell began straightway to share the indignation.

'We often do,' said Morris stoutly. 'We were going to the pictures together, but I didn't feel much like it, so after talking a bit, they went, as I said, and I came home.'

'And what time was this, did you say?' asked the detective.

'Well,' said Morris, allowing the least trace of annoyed irony to creep into his voice – no one but a fool or a guilty person could have ignored the trend of that question – 'I can tell you exactly, I think. I left here at 5.25 or so, caught the 5.41 at Charing Cross to Meadwell. I did that because my season ticket saved me my fare. Then I took the bus to Oldroyd's place. I must have got there about twenty past six. We stayed there together – no we didn't. I went out again to get a paper and some cigarettes, and as I got back Reddy had just turned up with his motor-bike. Then we stayed until eight, I should think. Then we separated, as I told you.'

The police officer was entirely convinced, rather against his will.

'Thank you, Mr Morris,' he said after a pause. 'I think that will do. Sorry to have troubled you, of course, but in the interests of justice, you know—'

'Don't mention it,' said Morris, withdrawing.

The interview had been worse than he had feared, but he had come through it triumphantly. He assured himself, not without quite good grounds, that he had accomplished a superb performance.

He came back into the composing room and looked about him. Reddy and Oldroyd were conversing in whispers in the far corner of the room. Clarence, Shepherd and the young traveller were, as was only to be expected, still discussing the tragedy, over by the window. No definite orders had come to them regarding their work – they could hardly be expected to leave off such an exciting discussion just on account of a few vague words from Mr Campbell brought by one so little in authority as Maudie. But the business of the office had to go on, and Morris could shoulder responsibility with an alacrity unknown to the others.

He went across and looked at the dated list of work to be delivered still pinned on Mr Harrison's desk.

'Is that stuff for the Scottish papers ready to send off, Shepherd?' he demanded.

'No,' said Shepherd blankly.

'Well, it's got to go off, hasn't it? Reddy, will you get hold of it and see that it's got into shape? There's a good chap. Mac will rave if it's not in the post by twelve. Shepherd, let's have those proofs of the marmalade ads. They've come in by now, haven't they? Oh, and Clarence, we want those other roughs ready for when the Adelphi man comes in this afternoon.'

The others looked at him stupidly for a moment. But they knew that the work had to be done, and they knew that they ought to be doing it. Morris, as the senior man in the room, had some slight ground for a display of authority, and in the last word, he was right in suggesting that they should start work. They moved slowly to their places; the deciding factor was Morris's hint that Mr Campbell would soon be asking about what was being done. Yet they had hardly settled down when the buzzer on Mr Harrison's desk uttered its low note. This time it was Morris who went into Mr Campbell's room to see what was wanted.

'Send Oldroyd in here,' said Mr Campbell; 'this gentleman wants to ask him a few questions.'

Morris had expected that, of course, but none the less it was a shock to him. Perhaps Oldroyd would falter. Probably he would not – but then the next step would be to send for Reddy. Could Reddy stand the strain? He was looking white and worried. Morris knew now the sensation of extreme pressing danger. The room seemed to go suddenly dark; he hesitated in his steps as though he experienced difficulty in finding his way back to the composing room. But he braced himself at the doorway. Not on any account must he show fear or worry. He pulled his big, solid shoulders back square. His brutal fatalist courage came to the rescue.

'Oldroyd,' he said pleasantly, 'the policeman wants to ask you a few questions as well.'

Oldroyd rose from his desk and turned towards him a face full of consternation; luckily his back was to the light.

'It's a good thing,' went on Morris, still speaking pleasantly, with his nerves keyed up to their highest pitch, 'it's a good thing

44

we were all together last night and can prove an alibi. I had to account for all my actions up to eight o'clock last night, and I suppose you'll have to as well. Go on in, sonny, and say that you couldn't have been up to any mischief, because you had your uncle Morris with you all the time.'

No one would ever have suspected Morris of being tactful, but the instant pressing danger brought out all the best in him. The gentle warning was conveyed without any suspicion arising in the minds of Clarence and the others. Oldroyd was steadied for the coming interview without any undue delay. He passed on to Mr Campbell's room: Morris fell wearily into his chair. This business was more exhausting than he had expected; but – it was this which was the most solid support to his waning strength – it *had* to be gone through. There was no backing out of a murder once the murder was committed. With death behind and life in front one could be sure of struggling on while it was possible still to struggle. He looked up and saw Reddy's white face turned towards him. Instantly he braced himself again. The man to whom the sight of panic among his subordinates is not merely not infectious, but is instead a steadying influence, is an ideal leader. Morris displayed ideal leadership when he forced himself to smile confidently across to Reddy. He reassured the wretched boy by his carefree demeanour.

Reddy, tortured with fear and remorse, did not know whether to admire or to hate the dark-haired villain who smiled at him so blandly. But it was wonderfully comforting, all the same, to see him sitting there looking as though he had not a trouble in the world. Reddy had at last achieved a sense of reality. It had not seemed possible to him that Mr Harrison would be killed, but now that had really happened he was able to realize that other unthinkable, horrible things could happen too: that John Reddy, for instance, could be hanged. Without Morris's continual reassurance the prospect drove him to blind panic. With it, it steadied him extraordinarily.

Oldroyd came back into the room; all eyes turned towards him.

'That's that,' he said, elaborately casual. The passing of the danger had gone to his head like liquor. 'What did you do last night? I? I was with my good friends Mr Morris and Mr Reddy. Blast his eyes! Does he think *we* did it?'

'Of course he doesn't,' cut in Morris abruptly. 'He's only got to ask these dam' fool questions out of routine. You could see that by the way he asks them.'

'That's so,' said Oldroyd solemnly. 'You are right, Mr Morris. Always right, as usual, Mr Morris.'

'Well, get on with those ads, now, anyway. This bally business is holding us up like billy-ho. What d'you think Mac'll say if we have to put a "reserved" ad. in the *Glasgow Advertiser*?'

A space in a newspaper bearing the large type announcement to the effect that: 'This space is reserved for So-and-So's Potted Meat Company', indicates that the company's advertising agents have sent in their advertisement too late for publication, and it is in consequence the most damning evidence of slackness in that office.

'Oh, God, listen to that!' went on Morris as the buzzer sounded again. 'I suppose they want someone else now.'

He was right. Mr Campbell and the police officer now demanded Reddy's presence.

'Reddy,' said Morris, standing in the doorway, 'Mac wants to see you.'

Reddy came over to him; he felt like a man going to death. Morris shut the door behind them.

'It's all right,' he said, low voiced. 'He isn't fierce. He hasn't got any suspicions. Really he hasn't. Just remember. You went home for your motor-bike, came along to Oldroyd's, met me outside, went in and talked and then went to the pictures. That's all.'

He patted Reddy on the shoulder, and somehow Reddy was supremely grateful for the contact. It made him feel much less isolated in the world. He went in feeling bolder than ever before, with Morris's last words fixed in his mind.

Morris was right. The police officer had no suspicions. He devoted only a cursory inspection and a few questions to this obviously harmless boy, and Reddy's embarrassment and confusion were put down to a not unnatural shyness. Mr Campbell had already given the police officer the best possible character for Reddy. And of all the people in the office Reddy, it appeared, had the smallest conceivable motive for the crime. Reddy never had a clear recollection of the interview, but it must have gone off well enough. Morris experienced immense relief when Reddy came back into the room and was able to smile weakly in response to the eager looks directed at him.

Until Clarence came back from his interview, too, and changed the subject, he answered quite intelligently the questions which were asked of him. Clearly he had survived the ordeal in the next room, and now there was nothing in his manner to rouse suspicion in the unthinking minds of Shepherd and of the elegant young traveller who was still lounging round the room.

This last young man felt himself a little aggrieved that Mr Harrison had got himself killed. He voiced his grievance to Morris.

'I suppose *my* work isn't important,' he said with devastating irony. 'You can turn to and work at those measly little ads., but you can't spare a minute to get out those examples we were talking about last night. Now that Mr Harrison's gone no one here knows what is important and what isn't.'

Morris put down his pen and stared at him. It took a moment or two for him to realize just what this fellow was talking about. Then he remembered, and he allowed the pent-up irritation within him free vent.

'Are you talking about those ads. for Nebuchadnezzar Cars?' he demanded. 'Do you really think, you poor idiot, that this office is going to waste a couple of days or so getting out sample ads. because you've got an idea you'd like to get their advertising? Talk sense. Why, even if you weren't the bloke approaching them we've got no more chance of getting it than – than we have of getting hell's advertising when hell sets up as a winter resort. You haven't got an idea in your head beyond motor-cars, just because your daddy lets you drive his out once a week. God lumme, this office doesn't run on half-million appropriations! Go and look through the papers and find the folk with two hundred a year to spend on advertising. Get them to give us the job, and we'll be grateful. Ten two hundred are a dam' sight better than one two thousand, an' the hell of a lot safer. Go out and get them – you haven't brought fresh work into this office for a couple of months or more. I'm sick of the sight of you. Hop it and give me a rest!'

The wretched youth had begun to wilt before the heat of this condemnation before Morris was half finished speaking; at the end of the speech he was reduced to utter feebleness, standing with his jaw dropped, wincing under the shrewd blows Morris dealt out to him. He might have replied had time been given to him, but any chance of that was obviated by the sound of Mr

Campbell's buzzer once more. Morris heaved himself up and went to see what it was this time.

Mr Campbell was seated at his desk with his rimless spectacles on and a kindly look in his short-sighted eyes.

'Ah, Morris,' he said. 'Sorry to bother you again when you've had such a disturbed morning.'

Morris made the inarticulate noise appropriate to a reply to an employer's apology.

'It's like this,' said Mr Campbell. 'After this very unfortunate business I must find someone to take Mr Harrison's place. He will have complete charge of the composing room – horrid word that, I always think. We're not compositors.'

'Yes, sir,' said Morris, his heart beating more violently than when he had shot Mr Harrison.

'You are the senior in there now,' went on Mr Campbell. 'I should at first have considered you too young for the position, although I like your work. But then I have just heard you telling young Lewis about the basis of this particular business. No, don't be surprised, because you know by now that I can hear most of what goes on in there. It's part of my job as your employer. Well, I liked what you had to say. And it would be a nuisance bringing in a new man to a job like that. Do you think you could take over Mr Harrison's position?'

'I think so, sir,' said Morris.

'Well, you can go back in there and tell them that you have it. You're getting four ten a week now, I think?'

'Yes, sir.'

'I paid Harrison eight. All the same, I won't give you that for a long time. But I'll make it five ten, starting from last Monday.'

'Thank you, sir.'

And with that Morris withdrew. It was the reward of success, the reward of a good plan well laid and well executed; a pound a week rise and promotion; money and power at once. Murder was both safer and more profitable than the receiving of bribes. Morris may possibly have had a twinge or two of conscience up to this time – it is hard to say whether he had or not – but from now on for certain he had none at all.

'Well, you blokes,' said Morris, back in the composing room, 'I've got Harrison's job. Sorry and all that, but that's how it is.'

The others looked at him. Reddy looked uncomprehending; Shepherd looked a little envious; Clarence cared nothing one

48

way or the other; Lewis looked utterly disconcerted; and Oldroyd was consumed with a fierce annoyance. This fellow had killed a man and had not merely got off scot free so far, but he had been given the best job in the office – the only one, too, to which Oldroyd, could aspire. Not merely that, but he had tied Oldroyd's hands so that the latter could not stir a finger against him. Oldroyd's slow north-country blood fairly boiled, not with righteous indignation, but with fury at being outwitted. It was worse still that he now would have to dissemble his fury, would have to kow-tow to his late accomplice, who was now lord of the composing room. Oldroyd pictured himself treating Morris with the deference with which he had previously treated Harrison, and he raged impotently at the thought.

Morris scanned their faces one at a time. He was superbly self-confident. There is nothing like a resounding success behind one to give one a good conceit of oneself.

'All right,' said Morris, 'let's get on with it. I want to see those roughs in half an hour's time, Clarence. Shepherd, get me the files of our ads. in the *Irish Times*. And have you got anything particular to do in here, Lewis?'

Lewis confessed that he had not, now that (so he began to continue) Morris had with vile prejudice decided against his pet plan.

'Right,' said Morris, cutting him short. 'Then this isn't the place for you. Your sphere of influence is the Great Outdoors. Go and find some business for us.'

Lewis went; and as he went Shepherd found the files Morris had asked for. He began to put them on Morris's table, but Morris checked him.

'I'll have them up here,' he said, and he indicated the late Mr Harrison's table, on the dais. It was an appropriate gesture.

To Morris there seemed nothing nightmarish, nothing unpleasant about the situation. Life was golden and hopeful. Both Reddy and Oldroyd felt the horror of sitting down to work with a murderer at their backs and in authority over them.

# CHAPTER VII

Mr Campbell thoroughly approved of the progress of his new deputy at the office. Harrison, Mr Campbell felt, had been too easy-going to keep his subordinates up to the mark, although that was just what Mr Campbell, an easy-going man himself, had paid him for. With Morris it was a different story. His new authority was intensely agreeable to him in his new successful mood. Promotion may have gone a little to his head, but years of service under Mr Harrison had most certainly taught him the weaknesses of Harrison's system – the chances it offered to his subordinates to waste time; the slack periods and the uneconomical rush times which it brought about; above all, he had been irritated times without number by Mr Harrison's constitutional inability to say no.

There was to be no more of that under Charlie Morris's regime. Messrs Reddy and Oldroyd and the new importation, Mr Howlett, were not allowed now to idle long hours away pretending to work. The office was, of course, full of the most fascinating newspapers and weekly periodicals, sent by publishers as voucher copies when the Universal Advertising Agency had bought space in them, and it was a huge temptation to read these things under the pretence of studying advertisements. Mr Morris arranged to put temptation out of the others' way by having all these piled up under his own eye. Slack times were to be filled in with starting new work, perhaps even as much as a week before it was wanted. And the suggestions which poured in upon him were decided upon instantly. Ninety times out of a hundred Mr Morris would say at once 'No good,' having heard the suggestion through. Nine times out of a hundred he would say, 'M'm. Might be something in it. Think it out better and bring it to me next week again.' Only once in a hundred times would he say, 'That seems all right. Let's have another look.' But when he said that a new advertisement was well on the way to being completed; and once the office had roughed it out it was extremely rare for Mr Campbell to veto it, while the client himself was usually as pleased as ever a client is with an agency's work – for what that recommendation is worth. Things were very different from under the sway of Mr Harrison, who would hum and haw for half a day over a new notion and invariably submitted to Mr Campbell twice as many suggestions as eventually found their way into the Press.

The new methods, however, did not endear Morris to the others. Shepherd, the ambitious office boy, simply hated Morris, for not only did Morris turn away with contempt from every one of his treasured suggestions (in an advertising office every member of the staff teems with artless ideas for the design of new advertisements), but also Morris knew to a minute how long it took to go from the office to all the places Shepherd had to go to, and Shepherd now found himself deprived of his long minutes of exquisite idling in the London streets. Clarence found that Morris's demands imposed a serious strain upon his artistic temperament. He did not like the way in which Morris expected work which could be done in an hour ready in an hour's time; still less did he like the offhand manner in which Morris condemned impressionist drawings and insisted on photographic realism. As for Lewis, the traveller, there were no bounds to his loathing for Morris, who persisted every day in demanding from him publicly an account of how he had spent his time, and who judged achievements not by the measure of dreams dreamed but by that of cold, hard figures of business brought in. Lewis, whose influential father was an old friend of Mr Campbell's, and whose mother was a distant relation, had no particular fear of losing his job. All the same, Morris's scathing public comments so pierced his sensitive skin that, unwilling, he actually began to work for his salary, and the more he worked the more his dislike of his tormentor increased.

Oldroyd felt the change worse still. He had been an old familiar of Morris, and would have been disconcerted by his promotion even if there had been no unusual event preceding it. It is hard to have to defer to a man with whom one has often spent long evenings chatting about every subject under the sun, and whose coffee one has often paid for, and who only last week was 'borrowing' cigarettes. Oldroyd would have been annoyed by Morris's cracking of the whip even solely on this account. But seeing that in addition Oldroyd knew that Morris was not above petty thievery it was more annoying still. Then there was Oldroyd's anger with Morris having lured him into legal complicity in his crime. The crime itself, after a day or two, did not prey so much on Oldroyd's mind. Try as he would, he could think no worse of Morris because the latter had killed a man. He could not regard him with awe or fear or disgust on that account. Yet it was highly irritating to Oldroyd to have Morris at his mercy on account of his knowledge and yet to be quite unable to make use of that knowledge, particularly when Morris was taking advantage of that fact to drive Oldroyd into an efficiency of work which was as tiresome as it was novel.

It was Reddy on whom the new state of affairs had the profoundest effect. Reddy, who always needed to admire someone, had alternated for some days between admiring Morris and hating him. At last he had come to hate him, and to fear him; Oldroyd's influence probably told in this respect. The Satanic cunning which Morris had displayed had first brought its feeling of distrust, and then had ruined all the boyish affection which Reddy had felt towards Morris on account of the latter's flamboyant personality. Reddy's feelings had changed very considerably. Once he had admired Morris's coarse good looks; now he was aware that they were coarse. Once he had thought Morris a man of determination; now he thought him merely unscrupulous. Once he had believed him to be a good fellow; now he knew him to be one who traded on that belief. The black crime on Morris's soul meant much to Reddy; Reddy would look at Morris's thick hands with disgusted fascination as the hands which had killed a man. Reddy was not at all in the state of mind which could produce good work, exact work, and original work, such as Morris was determined to exact from him.

And besides all this there was fear eating at the hearts of the two young men. Morris did not experience it. The interview with the police had gone off well. A puzzled coroner's jury, after two adjournments, had brought in the inevitable verdict of murder against persons unknown. Not an atom of evidence had been forthcoming. None of the pryings of the police had discovered anyone who might have desired Harrison's death, or who could have been near the scene of the murder when it was committed, not even though as a last resort they had interviewed Oldroyd's landlady, and had received her vague but reliable assurance that Oldroyd had not left the house before eight o'clock, and that he was certainly entertaining Morris and Reddy up to that time. Even had the chances of detection been much greater Morris would not have been afraid now – he was not that kind of criminal – but Reddy and Oldroyd were of different stuff. Oldroyd had been sick with fear ever since his landlady had told him of the visit of the police. At any moment he expected to feel the hand of arrest on his shoulder. His native stolidity enabled him to bear the strain without breaking down, but he felt it all the same.

Young Reddy was worse off still; he was on the verge of breaking down. He was tortured with remorse. The visit of Mrs Harrison to the office, when, tearful, clad in sombre mourning, she had come to interview Mr Campbell, had been horrible. Mr Campbell, good old soul, had done what he could, but all the same the little suburban home was to be sold up and the children were to go to charity schools, and Mrs Harrison was to be reduced to a miserable dependence upon relatives. Reddy's remorse was not alleviated even when he put two pound notes in an envelope, typed out Mrs Harrison's address with Maudie's typewriter and sent them off to her. But his fear was more acute even than his remorse. He had begun to sleep badly, and when he did sleep he dreamed horribly of arrest and trial and sentence and execution. He became noticeably thinner and paler. He wandered about his home like a ghost, worrying his mother distracted. Fortunately Mrs Reddy had the type of mind which attributed her son's obvious trouble to the machinations of a woman.

There came a day, only ten days after the murder, when the strain began to grow too great for Reddy. It was a Saturday morning, one of those Saturday mornings which are so particularly irritating because there is, on account of other firm's delays, a whole day's work to be compressed into it and no chance of enjoying Saturday amusements until it is done. Morris from his seat of power on his dais was dealing out work and encouragement and reproof lavishly to everyone in the room; but as much reproof as work, and not nearly as much encouragement. Pride of position was working powerfully still in Morris's soul.

'Haven't you got those lay-outs finished *yet*, Howlett?' he demanded. (Howlett was the new clerk.) 'Get a move on, sonny. There's lots more to be done after that. Clarence, come here a minute. D'you mean this bally woman to be cutting bread and butter or making wreaths? Cutting bread and butter? Then for God's sake make her look as though she likes it. We want folk to buy bread you know, not to be scared of it. I don't mind her looking sixty-five. That's not a bad idea as a change; every ad. in every paper has a bright young thing of twenty-five with three children nowadays. But she's got to look *happy*, man, *jolly*, as though this bread does her all the good in the world. Go and try again, and let's have it back in ten minutes. Now what do you want, Reddy?'

Reddy had come up to the table and was resting his hands on it, and his weight on his hands. His face was working horribly.

'I – I can't go on,' he said. He half whispered this, so that the others in the room would not hear; and as he spoke he looked over his shoulder to make certain that no one was listening.

'What on earth do you mean?' demanded Morris, but he dropped his voice as well. He looked at the tortured white face. There were actually tears in the blue eyes.

'I can't, I simply can't,' said Reddy.

Morris drew his brows together in the fierce scowl which Reddy had been dreading.

'No, don't!' wailed Reddy. 'I want to talk to you. I must, I tell you.'

Reddy had come to him for sympathy; perhaps it would be better stated that what Reddy wanted was a fresh transfusion of courage which he knew Morris could instil in him if he liked. For Morris to display the contempt of and annoyance at his weakness to which Reddy knew he was exposing himself would be the last straw. The fact that Reddy had come for moral aid to Morris, whom he hated, was proof enough of Reddy's need.

Morris felt this dimly. Anyway, he did not allow his annoyance at the incident to overmaster him. He tried to bring a hint of kindliness into his tone.

'Feeling a bit done?' he said. 'Working too hard?'

Both of them knew that work had almost nothing to do with Reddy's present condition, but Reddy agreed.

'See here,' said Morris. 'Go out and get yourself a cup of coffee. Take some of these papers to read. You'll feel better after a bit.'

'Thank you,' said Reddy, and he was really grateful. 'But I *must* see you, I *must* talk to you about – about – a'

'Oh, all right,' said Morris. 'I'll see you at lunch-time. We'll have lunch together. Go out and get a coffee, and come back when you feel like it.'

Reddy went, and Morris shook off the memory of the unpleasant incident as best he could while he plunged anew into the mass of work on his table. But it recurred to him repeatedly; the white worried face came up before his eyes with tiresome iteration even while he dealt with matters of consuming interest. It was half an hour before Reddy came back again, slipping quietly into the room and crossing unobtrusively to his place.

The work was finished somehow. Clarence was packed off, much to his delight, at a quarter past one, and Howlett followed him. Shepherd was given a mass of letters to post and told he need not return. Mr Campbell came in wearing his hat and coat.

'I'm off now, Morris,' he said; 'and I've told the girls they can go. Nothing you want them for, is there?'

'No, sir. Goodbye, sir,' said Morris.

So the three of them were left alone in the composing room – Oldroyd bent over an intricate job of filing, Reddy fidgeting restlessly in his chair, and Morris seated at his telephone. He was doing proof correction over that instrument – always a ticklish operation.

'Now look at the bottom right-hand corner,' he said – he held a proof copy of an advertisement appearing in a Sunday newspaper tomorrow in his hand, and presumably the invisible compositor at the other end of the wire held another. 'That "H" beside the woman's foot. Is that bad type or a bad pull? A bad pull? You're sure? All right, then. And the last line of all, "Buy one on Monday." You've used the wrong fount. We asked for Caslon Old Face, and that's not Caslon. Oh, yes, we did. I've got the lay-out in front of me while I'm speaking to you. Well, can you get it right if you change the type? Or shall I wait for a second proof? Yes, I know what time you go to press. But it's not our fault if you send the proof at the last minute like this. Well, mind you get it right, old man. You don't want our Mr Campbell complaining to your boss, do you? All right, then. Goodbye. Yes, goodbye.'

He hung the receiver on its hook with a sigh of relief.

'That's the last job I've got to do, thank God,' he announced. 'What about you, Oldroyd? Nearly finished?'

'Just on,' said Oldroyd, snapping down the clasps viciously. Huddersfield Town were playing in London that Saturday, and it was now too late for him to get to the match in time.

'Reddy and I are going to lunch together,' said Morris. 'Coming?'

'What's the idea?' asked Oldroyd cautiously. He was always suspicious now of any suggestion coming from Morris.

'Don't ask me,' said Morris. 'I don't know. This is Reddy's idea. He's afraid to lunch by himself, or something.'

At which unkind speech Reddy felt more distressed than ever. He looked blindly at their unsympathetic faces.

'You beasts!' he said. 'Yes, both of you. You – you—' But Reddy did not possess the eloquence, especially at that moment, which could give even a sketchy idea of the tangled state of his emotions. His friendlessness and his peril left him unnerved. He actually began to sob, and at the sight of that Morris held back the testy contempt he was about to express.

'Oh, pull yourself together, sonny,' said Morris soothingly, 'and tell us what's the matter. You'll feel better then. What's the trouble?'

'Oh,' said Reddy unhappily, 'it's just – it's just – the awfulness of all this. What's going to happen?'

'Why, nothing, of course,' said Morris, but he broke off his speech there for an instant while he peered into Mr Campbell's room, and darted out into the corridor to make sure there was no one within earshot.

'We're as safe as houses,' went on Morris, returning. 'No one's got any idea about the business at all. I can't see what you're worrying about.'

'Oh, it's not only that,' said Reddy; 'there's Mrs Harrison and – and – everything.'

By 'everything' Reddy meant his own lonely, troubled conscience.

'Where's it going to end?' asked Reddy pitifully.

'End?' asked Morris in return. 'End? It's not going to end, I hope. There can't be any end to this business for us.'

By that speech, which Morris meant to be reassuring, he only accentuated the horror in Reddy's face. Reddy saw extending before him a life of endless fear and endless remorse.

'I can't bear it,' said Reddy. 'I can't. And I won't. I'll – I'll—'

'You'll what?' asked Morris sharply. The weakness of his

late brilliant plan was beginning to reveal itself. Morris's good fortune, Morris's life itself, depended on the constancy of this frail creature.

'My mother thinks there's something wrong,' said Reddy. He said that in preference to confessing his half-formed design of unburdening his troubles upon her. Reddy was not used either to a guilty conscience nor to having secrets from his mother.

'Your mother thinks so, does she?' said Morris grimly, and looked at Oldroyd. Oldroyd at the moment was more curious than frightened. He saw the implication in Reddy's last speech, and he was curious to know how Mr Too-clever Morris proposed to escape from this dilemma.

'What have you told her up to now?' demanded Morris.

'Nothing,' bleated Reddy, 'as yet.'

He caught Morris's furious eye, and continued unhappily:

'Really I haven't, Morris. But you don't seem to care what I feel like, and I thought – I thought – well, I couldn't go on like this by myself.'

That bad temper of Morris's was up in arms by now. He was furiously angry with this weak-kneed ninny who was imperilling everything. But he saw that he would have to restrain himself, to coax and to comfort. It was worse than dealing with a girl. With a girl there was nothing much at stake, and there were hundreds of other girls just as good to be had for the asking. But Morris had only one neck, and he did not want that dislocated because of a babbling fool. He appealed to reason.

'Oh, dash it, old man,' he said, 'you're not by yourself. We're all in this with you. It's all our faults, you know that. We're standing by you, and you ought to stand by us. You can't do any good by telling anyone, not a scrap of good. You feel worried now, and you tell your mother. Then she feels worried and tells someone else. The fat's in the fire then. We'll all be for it straight away. For God's sake, Reddy, do you *want* to be – hanged?'

'No,' said Reddy and paused. 'But – but—'

What Reddy wanted to say was that, although he did not want to be hanged, he wanted possibly even less to be condemned to spend the rest of his life with this secret locked, unconfided, in his breast. And Morris saw that the appeal of reason was wanting. A man who can continue to say 'but'

57

when faced with the prospect of hanging is not to be reasoned with. Morris screwed down his anger a little farther and tried to appeal to sentiment. Yes, it was far worse than dealing with a girl.

'But you can't let us down, old man. We've trusted you, you know, Oldroyd here and I have. We've put our lives, we've put everything in your hands. You wouldn't let your pals down like that, would you?'

That clearly had some effect, and Morris continued hastily:

'I don't know why you seem to hate me nowadays, old man. I thought you used to like me a bit once.'

(Even Morris the unscrupulous felt a little ashamed somehow at using this cheap appeal. But it was the only way.)

'It was because of that that I trusted you,' he went on. 'And Oldroyd here. You're still pals with him, aren't you? We're friends together. Let's stick to one another. Here, let's shake hands on it.'

It was a sentimental, silly situation; one of the kind Morris would hoot and jeer at inwardly if he came across it in a book or a play. But it suited the needs of the case. Reddy's hand came out, and Morris clasped it firmly, looking Reddy straightly in the eyes.

'There, that's fine. Now shake hands with Oldroyd, too.'

The little ceremony had an absurdly devivifying effect on Reddy; a gesture meant so much to the ridiculous, sentimental boy.

'And now let's come and have some lunch and forget our troubles,' said Morris.

Morris found comforting Reddy much more arduous and tiresome than planning murder.

# CHAPTER VIII

Mrs Morris sat by the fireside in the house at the top of the hill waiting for her husband to come back from the office. Because she was waiting for her husband, which implies that her husband was not in the house at the moment, she was sitting in the only armchair. She would move out of it when he arrived; despite the fact that she enjoyed quarrelling with him, she was imbued with enough of the traditional working-class respect for the wage-earner to allow him the best of everything available without question. And at the moment Mrs Morris's respect for her husband was considerably increased. Had he not brought her the glad news that his wages had been increased by ten shillings a week, and was he not passing on seven and sixpence of that increase to her for the house-keeping? A worse husband would have kept the secret of that rise in wages to himself and spent the money on the foolery men do spend money on. She was proud of her husband's success. Already he was earning more than her own father had ever earned. It had been a bit of a struggle so far to manage with a whole house to themselves, but things would be easier now. Always until she had married, Mrs Morris and her family had lived in houses in which either she and her family were lodgers or in which her family took in lodgers. Living only two in a room, as they did at present, meant better conditions than Mrs Morris had usually known; her husband had climbed above the station in life in which he was born, and was a man of achievement in consequence. Mrs Morris felt really kindly towards her husband when she thought of the fine little joint she had in readiness for tomorrow's Sunday dinner. It was good to have food like that to set before Molly and little John. She heard at last his key in the door and quietly transferred herself and her darning to the other, less comfortable, chair.

He came in slow of step and weary, as she was growing used to seeing him.

'Had your dinner?' she asked.

'Yes,' he said, and sat down in the armchair. They had nothing much to say to each other, these two.

Morris proceeded to light a cigarette, and he sat smoking and gazing into the fire. Tired though he was, a new idea was fermenting in his brain. The exalted mood of high creative construction was close upon him, even though he did not yet recognize the symptoms. His wife, at least, realized that he was in a self-absorbed study, and she knew that it would be hard work to quarrel with him, even if she wanted to; and she was not particularly anxious to do so. Half a dozen recent quarrels, the news of the rise in wages and the purchase of that exceptional joint for tomorrow had brought a sufficiency of colour into her life for the present. She sat and darned placidly.

But the quiet of the room could not last long. The door into the garden opened and someone looked in round the edge of it. It was Molly, and as soon as she saw her father she came scuttling into the room, leaving, of course, the door open behind her.

'Daddy,' she said, 'dad-*dee!*'

She shook his arm.

'What's the matter with you?' demanded Morris ungraciously.

Molly had no answer ready; all she wanted to do was to attract her father's attention; she never seemed able to learn that nowadays her father did not want to be disturbed by her.

'We're digging,' said Molly, with a wave of her hand towards the garden. 'Johnny and me are. In the garding.'

John Morris, aged two, made his appearance at the door at that moment, wrapped in the overcoat and muffler of which he was so proud. Morris foresaw his peaceful afternoon ruined by the attentions of his children.

'My God, what a draught!' he said, glaring at the door.

Mrs Morris got up and shut it.

'You didn't ought to leave the door open like that, Molly,' she said; and as she spoke the wild yells of John Morris, who could not open the door yet, came most penetratingly into the room.

'Bless these kids!' said Morris irritably. 'Can't you keep 'em quiet?'

'They were quiet enough before you came in,' snapped Mrs Morris. She took Molly by the arm, and such was the association of the ideas of being irritable and holding the little girl that she shook her quite unintentionally. Molly's howls began to blend with the muffled sound of John's sorrow outside.

'Oh, my God!' said Morris.

'Be quiet!' snapped Mrs Morris at Molly.

'Oh, take 'em out, take 'em away,' said Morris. 'Here!'

He dived into his trousers pocket and produced a sixpence, which he handed to his wife.

'Ooh!' said Molly.

'Take 'em out and buy 'em sweets or something. Do anything you like as long as they're away from here.'

Mrs Morris would have been glad to refuse for many reasons, but there were still more reasons which forced her to obey. There would be no controlling Molly if that young woman saw the golden prospect of sixpennyworth of sweets torn from her. And there was something about her husband's manner these days which told her it would be well to obey him. She took the coin a little ungraciously, for she had in her mind's eye a picture of the walk down to the shops and, worse than that, the walk back again, pushing that heavy boy in his chair up that dreadful hill. But all the same she put on her hat and coat, taking them off the pegs in the hall, and she collected the children, and she started. Morris, wandering aimlessly round the house, looked out of the front window and saw them half-way down the hill. Molly was skipping fantastically at her mother's side, wildly excited at the thought of sweets. John was in his push-chair, waving the wooden spade which his mother had been unable to induce him to leave behind. Mary herself was walking slowly, bracing back against the slope of the hill in a manner which her high heels did not render graceful, and holding on tightly to the push-chair in front of her. It crossed Morris's mind that if she were to let go there was nothing to stop John, push-chair and all, hurtling down the street to the main road at the bottom, to the trams and the buses and the lorries.

Morris, now that he had the house to himself, could not settle down; perhaps that was why he had wanted the house to himself. He prowled restlessly round the house. He sat down for a few minutes by the fire, but only for a few minutes; soon he was on his feet again, walking about. There was a strange fermenting of thoughts and ideas within him, but he still could not recognize the premonitory symptoms of the descent upon him of inspiration. What was worrying him most was the revelation of how weak was his position (which should have been so strong) on account of Reddy's ridiculous behaviour. Morris knew instinctively that the boy was quite capable of blurting out the whole business. Morris felt that he himself could probably keep Reddy from this suicidal act by the force of his own encouragement for a while, but there were difficulties, actual and potential, in the way. He could never be certain of keeping Reddy up to the mark. He might fall ill, or Reddy might – Reddy probably would, from the look of him.

Anyway, he could not keep it up for ever; something would have to be done about it sooner or later, and in that case sooner would be much better than later. The question was what was there he could do?

More than that, Morris was in his usual condition of high annoyance. He ought to have been annoyed with himself for not having foreseen this possibility earlier, but naturally he did not allow himself to be; that side of the picture did not present itself to his mind's eye. Instead, he was furiously angry with Reddy. The weak-nerved little swine appeared intensely objectionable to him, and the prospect of having to continue to coax and cajole the boy, of making allowance for his absurd whim, simply infuriated Morris. And in this special case so much depended on keeping the boy up to the mark; all Morris's new won promotion depended on it, the success which was at last to his hand – all this was as important to Morris as his life itself, which was also in the balance. Morris could picture financial ruin with all its horrors easily enough, for he had encountered it before; arrest and execution, on the other hand, were merely vague unpleasant possibilities to be avoided at all costs, but not nearly as vividly detailed in his mind.

Morris's caged prowlings round the house brought him up against the mirror which stood over the sitting-room mantelpiece. He checked himself and looked into it. He examined curiously the big virile face which looked back at him. There was the abundant dark hair with a bit of a wave in it, the irregular forehead, the intense brown eyes under their thick brows. The thick hooked nose betrayed an admixture of Jew in his ancestry – Morris knew that – and the hint was confirmed by the olive tint in his cheeks. The full lips and the heavy jaw did not help to make his face a handsome one, although Morris, peering at himself, was quite satisfied. He might have been better looking, just as his career might have been more brilliant, but in each case the full achievement was something to be rather proud of.

To have climbed, with no education except what an elementary school had thrust upon him, to his present position was quite distinguished. To earn five ten a week and have five men working under him – and one of them a toff from a good school – was more than his old man himself could boast. Morris could see himself climbing higher yet, to a position of vast power and profit in the advertising world. He knew, he *knew*, that he had good ideas on the subject of advertising, and that he had a force of personality which would make itself felt. If the Universal Agency offered him too little scope he would leave it, later – or he would make it grow while he grew

62

with it. He could see himself making a hundred thousand a year out of advertising before long; it was there for someone to make. And yet all these glorious possibilities were dependent on the whim of a white-faced boy whose moods were as flighty as a woman's!

Morris beat one hand into the other with rage as he thought of this. If only something would happen to stop the boy's mouth! He would stop it himself gladly, he decided, but—The thick hands which could strangle the boy easily clenched hard as he realized the difficulties of that course. Perhaps that was the first time that Morris definitely came to consider the advantages which would follow Reddy's death. Death, Morris realized without calculation, for such was his simple realist's mind, was the only thing that would make Reddy safe. In that case, seeing that there was advantage to be gained from Reddy's death, Morris would have been glad to know of Reddy's death. No other consideration entered into the balance at all. Morris did not care in the least whether Reddy lived or died except from this particular point of view of his own advantage.

It is perfectly true that Morris came more readily to examine the advantages which this would bring about in consequence of the killing of Harrison. One violent death having already occurred made it easier to begin to make calculations based on a second. It helped Morris to start considering the matter, and the anger he felt towards Reddy carried the debate a stage farther. One life more or less did not matter much to Morris; and he had progressed so far since Harrison's murder that he had begun to look upon death as the suitable recompense for anyone who crossed his path. Morris was becoming a dangerous man. Idle expressions such as 'an acquired taste for blood' are not entirely pointless. They convey a definite possibility rather inexactly. Killing for killing's sake is extraordinarily rare, but killing for quite inadequate motives is much more usual.

All the same Morris, contemplating Reddy's death, thought the matter over cautiously. An unexplainable tragedy such as had disposed of Harrison would be highly dangerous. Two mysterious deaths of people employed in the same small office would direct inquiry towards the few people working in that office, and Morris, with knowledge now of the thinness of the ice over which he had skated in the Harrison affair, could not possibly trust himself to arrange an event which would not yield evidence to the searching investigation over a narrowed field which would follow. He had no lack of confidence in his own powers, but he sorely misdoubted the possible effect of bad luck and unforeseen circumstances. So that the unexplainable, motiveless type of murder was too dangerous to repeat.

Morris, by grasping this essential fact, saved himself from many of the pitfalls which beset most criminals. Too slavish repetition of a previous successful crime has brought many a man to the gallows – George Joseph Smith, who drowned his brides, is the standard example; fortunately, there are few criminals original enough or careful enough to vary their methods.

Compelled, therefore, to think of some new device, Morris, now that his contemplation of Reddy's death was in full swing, began to think of how Reddy could die without suspicion being roused which could turn in his direction. Suicide? Morris considered that possibility quite seriously. A deft exertion of his personality might possibly, even probably, induce Reddy to kill himself, but there was always the chance of farewell letters and things like that – Reddy was so damnably unreliable that Morris could see himself trusting that the boy would not write and give the whole game away first; especially Morris, in his contempt for that wavering character, could not credit him with the amount of resolution necessary to carry the thing through to the end. He would probably make a botch of it.

On the other hand, Morris could perhaps try to arrange Reddy's death in such a way that someone else would be accused of the crime. Morris went into the infinite ramifications of this possibility with his usual thoroughness. But he could not come to any satisfactory decision. He did not know enough about Reddy's home life to be able to plan well; the data were insufficient. And that sort of thing would call for much planning and ground-baiting beforehand. Even then any scheme he could build up would be a shaky, rickety affair at best, he felt. There would be too many weak points, even if he spent months over the business, and at present he could not evolve even the germ of an idea upon which to build.

Morris at this point almost began to leave off considering the affair at all, despite the faint feeling of disappointment that would have brought. The surge of creative zeal within him was either illusory or wasted, he began to decide. He could think of no foundation on which to build up a plan for Reddy's unsuspicious death.

Then it was that the germ of the new idea came to him. For a few minutes he did not realize what was happening, but immediately afterwards, in less than ten seconds, he had evolved the whole scheme complete save for the minor details. Morris felt the warm flush of blood which he had known before, when Harrison's conversation with Maudie had given him the hint he had needed. It was the instant of creation; for a space Morris's mind, although a running river of thought, was in superb working order, logical and clear. He paced up and down again. Now that the main idea had come to him it was easy enough to work out details; not merely details of execution, which seemed to evolve themselves in his mind without conscious effort, but the equally important circumstantial details. Satisfied for the moment, he broke off his line of thought to follow out developments and consequences; they too, as far as he could see, were satisfactory enough. Turning the whole plan over and over in his mind, he could find no flaw, no objection. It called for an effort of self-control not to decide in favour of the scheme at once. His trust in this marvellous new power of his was such that he was on the point of making up his mind that the plan was exactly right; but he was cautious enough to control himself and put it on one side in his mind for further subconscious consideration before committing himself to it – Morris was of that obstinate breed which, once decided upon a course of action, find it impossible to draw back. And one disastrous failure – that of the scheme for extracting bribes from the Adelphi Studio – had taught Morris the need for caution. Morris was a far more dangerous criminal in consequence.

When Mrs Morris and the children returned the mid-November darkness was falling, but Morris had not yet lighted the gas. He was sitting by the dying fire in the twilight, but it was instantly obvious to Mary that his irritable mood had gone, even though a rather abstracted one had replaced it. He took John on his knee, while Molly climbed on the arm of his chair, and he listened to their talk with some show of intelligence while Mary lit the gas and drew the curtains and bustled about preparing tea. He ate the sticky sweets which John and Molly pressed upon him, and he dandled John on his knee in the manner of any ordinary father. Some of the sixpence he had given Mary had been spent not on sweets for the children, but on crumpets for their father – a delicacy which had been all too unusual in the days before Morris received his one pound a week increase in salary. Morris liked them; he was a man of greedy appetite. It would have been obvious to anyone who saw him eating those crumpets – leather ones awash with melted butter, several of them, and washing them down with cup after cup of strong stewed tea, that there was one obvious reason at least for his frequent bad temper. Not that bad temper was at all in evidence at the moment. On the contrary, such was his good temper that he promised that on the morrow, if it were fine, he would take the children out for a walk in the morning, which meant extraordinary condescension on his part. Mrs Morris could hardly believe her ears when she heard him suggest it, and beamed on him delightedly when she realized that he was making a genuine offer.

## CHAPTER IX

On Sunday morning Morris woke at his usual time, and in response to what usually woke him – the noise of John and Molly playing in the next room. For a moment he experienced the usual depression, which turned to sleepy elation as he remembered that it was Sunday and that there was no need to get up immediately. With a murmured 'Bless those kids,' he turned over drowsily on to his other side to sleep again. It was a blessedly peaceful moment. He was just drifting off to sleep again when recollection came to him. He had to make a decision; the sudden shock of remembering this had him wide awake instantly. He began to go through his plan again, bit by bit, testing it, until he reached its consummation, and from there he proceeded onwards seeking out possible unpleasant consequences. In the end he decided that the plan was sound. Then in the laziness of Sunday morning he had to decide whether or not to carry it through.

Mary, dozing blissfully, suddenly began to appreciate the fact that her husband had turned towards her, and put out inquiring little hands to him under the bedclothes; but he ignored her, and when she persisted he hunched over again on to his other side so as to be free to think. For his plan to work really well called for the execution of it on a Sunday, so that if he did not act today he would have to wait a week, and a week might be too long. Another essential part of the plan was the Sunday morning walk with the children, which would be a tiresome business. But on the other hand, in readiness for his decision, he had announced yesterday that he would take them, and it would be nearly as tiresome in its consequences to say that he had changed his mind. Young Reddy's life see-sawed in the balance as Morris lay idly in bed debating these factors for and against. Then the balance swayed down definitely and irrevocably as Morris arrived at a final decision. And having done so, Morris was able now to drift off again into a comfortable doze; he had that keen brain of his under better control now and he could restrain its activity better – largely, of course, because there was not so much exciting novelty about making plans now.

At breakfast it would have been difficult for anyone to discern any real difference in him. There might perhaps be an air of decision about him, a hard line or two round his mouth, which was not usually apparent. But he was not particularly abstracted to all seeming. Yet he may have appeared just a trifle anxious to start off in good time for that Sunday walk with the children.

'Where are we going, Daddy?' asked Molly as they left the house.

'Park,' replied Morris briefly. The air of decision was much more noticeable now, and he looked at his watch, and in consequence of the information gathered thereby he quickened his step, so that John in his push-chair felt he was really flying, while Molly had to trot beside him almost as fast as her short legs could carry her.

'Are we *really* goin' to the park, Daddy?' asked Molly. 'Oh, *Daddy!*'

For the park was a long way away, in a northerly direction (towards the district where Reddy lived), and it was so far away that Mrs Morris had rarely found time to take the children there. They had come to look upon it as a rarely attainable paradise.

Over the main road they went; they had to wait quite a long time before they could cross because there was so much traffic. There were plenty of motor-cars setting out for the country, because this was a fine Sunday although a November one, and there were the usual trams and buses – the road was quite thick with traffic; and, although Morris fumed a little at the delay, he found the presence of so much traffic very gratifying somehow. Once across, they hurried by the side streets as fast as Morris could walk comfortably, and much faster than Molly could walk comfortably. But Morris strode along unheeding; he paid no attention and made no reply to the few conversational openings which Molly found breath to make. Then they came to another main road, and when they had crossed that and walked a few yards up the next road they reached a big iron gate with stone pillars, and, passing through, the whole wonderful view of the park was opened to them. John began to sing, and even Molly forgot how hot and tired she was.

But even in this lovely place Morris still appeared to be in a hurry, and he would not sit down on a seat and rest as Molly wanted him to do, nor would he go on to the grass and unstrap John from his chair as John wanted him to do. He hurried along the winding gravel paths, looking ahead as if he was seeking someone or something. Molly wanted to stop and look at the ducks being fed, but he did not bestow a glance upon them. They hurried round the lake with the rowing boats on it so fast that Molly could not see nearly as much as she wanted to see. The paths were full of Sunday morning people, and from every point of vantage Morris looked eagerly along the groups, as though searching for someone.

And then Morris ceased to hurry. He abandoned his rapid stride in favour of a gait much more leisurely and suitable for a fine Sunday morning.

'What did you say, dear?' he asked, bending down a little to catch Molly's childish comments on the beauties of the park.

Molly did not notice this magnificent condescension; she was merely pleased at at last having attention paid to her. Morris listened attentively; he took one hand off the back of the push-chair for Molly to hold, and the three of them went on very gently along the gravel path, with Molly holding her father's hand and chattering to him gaily. They made quite a pretty, leisurely picture; so it certainly appeared to the young fellow and his father who were approaching in the opposite direction.

'Why, it's Morris!' said Reddy suddenly. He turned a little pale at seeing him thus unexpectedly.

'Hallo, old man,' said Morris. 'Good morning, Mr Reddy.'

He beamed at them in the pleasant winter sunshine.

'Good morning, sir,' said Mr Reddy. He had good old-fashioned ideas about being cordial towards his son's superior in the office.

'Isn't it a beautiful day?' said Morris. 'Taking the air, sir?'

'Yes, my son usually comes for a walk here with his old father on Sunday mornings,' said Mr Reddy, telling Morris exactly what he knew already.

'And I usually come for a walk here with my young son,' said Morris. 'John, Molly, say "How do you do" to Mr Reddy. And this is your Uncle John. That's your name, isn't it, Reddy?'

The children smiled shyly at the two strange men.

'And how old are you, Molly?' asked Mr Reddy.

'I'm nearly five,' whispered Molly.

The conversation followed stereotyped lines, with Reddy, rather pale and uneasy, in the background.

'Well, I must be moving on, I think,' announced Morris at length.

'Perhaps Mr Morris would come and have a cup of tea at home with us this afternoon, Johnny?' suggested Mr Reddy, still carefully cultivating a friendly attitude towards his son's official superior.

'Thank you,' said Morris; 'but I always spend Sunday afternoon with the wife and kiddies. Why don't you come over to tea, Reddy? Run over on the little mo'bike?'

Reddy did not specially want to; at the same time he had already learned by experience that an idle afternoon was terribly hard on his nerves. He hesitated visibly.

'You haven't got anything else to do, have you, Johnny?' asked Mr Reddy.

'No, Father.'

'Then of course you had better go.'

'That's fine,' said Morris. 'About four, old man?'

'All right,' said Reddy with an ill grace.

The party separated at the park gate, the children waving goodbye to the two Reddys. Then Morris directed his way homeward again, striding out with the old vigour, Molly panting along at his side, and his pose as a kindly father completely vanished once more. He could picture the conversation going on at that moment between Reddy's father and Reddy; the old man accentuating the need for Reddy to be on the best of terms with Morris, and Reddy sulkily agreeing. The essential preliminaries of the plan had been accomplished marvellously well; now – there was roast mutton at home, and Morris was hungry. He did not even pause to leave the children outside a public-house while he went in for an appetizer. He hurried the children back along the side streets, over the main road and up the steep hill again to his home. A man of Morris's calculating and obstinate mind did not feel the stress of waiting very much. He ate his dinner with considerable appetite.

Mrs Morris was perfectly delighted with everything: with her husband's appetite, with the good food she had bought for her children and with the news that Reddy was coming to tea. He had paid flying visits once or twice before, and she was very struck with his nice gentlemanly manners and his cultivated accent. Mrs Morris did not know many men who would offer her a chair before sitting down themselves.

After dinner Morris was even able to doze for a time in his armchair, digesting his mutton and cabbage and baked potatoes, and stewed apples and synthetic custard. It was not merely that he was a man of steady nerve; it was largely because of a self-confidence amounting to vanity that he was able to await a crisis so calmly. But even he, once digestion was completed, grew just a little uneasy and restless and paced about the house for a while just before four o'clock. Then a motor-bicycle came roaring up the hill and stopped with a popping of the exhaust outside the gate, and Molly came running to her daddy with the announcement, 'He's come, Daddy.' Visitors to Morris's home were sufficiently rare to be exciting.

'Come on in, old man,' said Morris at the door. 'What about the old bus? Better not leave it in the road with all these kids about. That's the idea, stick it inside the gate. Here we are, then. You know Mrs Morris, don't you, old man?'

Morris's sham-bluff garrulity was not due to any nervous qualms about the immediate future. It was merely evidence of a conscious lack of good breeding. Reddy was brought into the sitting-room and the best chair was pushed forward for him, with Morris talking effusively, Mrs Morris wearing her best blouse, all of a pleased flutter, and the children, rather shy, standing near the door solemnly watching it all. All this fuss about a single visitor left Reddy rather bored and uncomfortable. He tried not to be snobbish, but he could not help noticing more than usual the traces of Morris's council school accent, and the unconsciously deferential tone in Mrs Morris's voice, and the awkward bad manners of the children. Tea, sitting up at the table, with thick bread and butter, and whispered reproofs darted at the children, who were reverting, as children will, from shyness to rowdiness, was more of an ordeal still. And when after tea Morris led him again to the fireside with the obvious intention of making further polite conversation Reddy was very bored and uncomfortable indeed.

It was even worse when Morris went out of the room and left him with Mrs Morris, who had no conversation at all. Morris was gone for quite ten minutes, and the interval seemed like hours to Reddy, while Mrs Morris sat opposite him painstakingly trying to make conversation and failing utterly. Some years of housekeeping on a four pounds ten a week income make a very poor training for acting as hostess to a good-looking young man twenty-one years of age and of good family. Mrs Morris was thoroughly uncomfortable as well by the time Morris came back into the sitting-room.

'You've been away a long time,' said Mrs Morris fretfully. 'What on earth have you been up to?'

'Oh, just looking after one or two things,' answered Morris, and the answer was deemed satisfactory, although anyone who paid serious consideration to the matter would have found it hard to have named any 'things' Morris might want to 'look after,' or any particular reason why he should want to look after them just then. But Mrs Morris had long ago abandoned any attempt to account for her husband's actions.

Young Reddy rose to go, and Mrs Morris made no effort to detain him. Although the prospect of a visit from a nice young man was always so stimulating, Mrs Morris found the actual event rather exhausting, and was glad when it came to an end. Morris himself was a little more pressing.

'Have you got to go, old man?' he said. 'That's a pity. I was looking forward to a long evening with you. It's a girl, I suppose, who demands your presence? No? We have to take your word for it, I suppose. Molly! John! Uncle John is going now.'

The two children came hurrying down the stairs; they were anxious not to miss the starting of that massive motor-bicycle

71

which stood in the front garden and which savoured of hot oil in the most heavenly fashion.

It had fallen dark a little before. Reddy turned on his acetylene lamps and wheeled the machine out into the road at the corner, facing down the terrible slope. A new and delightful smell of acetylene came to the children's noses before Reddy struck a match and lighted his lamps. Everyone regarded him solemnly. Anyone who could have spared a glance for Morris might have seen hard lines round his tight-shut lips, giving him the same expression of savage resolution as he had worn at the moment when Harrison was shot.

Reddy said his farewells to the group; he shook hands with Mrs Morris, and he chucked Molly under the chin in the awkward fashion to be expected of a young man with no experience of children. He sought out John's hand and shook it.

'Goodbye, John,' he said.

'Goodbye,' piped John.

'Goodbye, old man,' said Morris. There was a flat kind of tone in his voice.

Reddy jerked up the stand to its catch, straddled the machine and thrust at the kick-starter. The engine broke into a roar. Reddy thrust once or twice with his feet, and as the bicycle began to run down the slope he put in his clutch. The clutch engaged for two or three yards while he adjusted the throttle controls, and then suddenly the note of the engine rose to a loud clamour which indicated that it was running free. Reddy's hand went automatically to the clutch. It hung curiously loose in its notch. It was a full two seconds before Reddy could realize that the drive to the back wheel was out of order. Actually the spring link of the driving chain had been weakened in some fashion – perhaps by unscrewing the nuts retaining it – and the chain now lay in the road fifty yards behind him. Reddy switched off the engine. He was already flying down that fearful hill; the manner in which the bicycle leaped at a bump in the road told him how fast he was travelling. He stretched out his fingers and gripped his brakes, first the rear one and then the front. And first the one lever and then the other came up at his touch without any show of resistance. The rods were pulling through the nuts at the points of adjustment; those nuts, too, must have worked loose somehow. By this time the bicycle was only a hundred yards from the main road, a hundred yards of steep hill in which to gather further velocity; and the main road across the foot of the hill was thronged with motor-cars returning from a Sunday in the country, and with motor-buses, and with charabancs, and with tramcars. The bicycle covered that hundred yards in four seconds; just long enough for Reddy to realize with a gasp of fear the fate that lay before him. He felt icy cold; perhaps the strain of the last ten days had its effect on his nerve, too. He was sitting dazed and inert in the saddle as the motor-bicycle dashed silently and without warning into the mass of cross traffic. There was no possible hope for him; perhaps there would have been none had he kept his nerve. The bicycle rebounded with a crash from the side of a tramcar and a motor-car, although travelling at quite a moderate speed, pulled up too late. Several drivers had shouted in the flurry of the moment. They were silent now as they pulled up and got out to discover what damage had been done. A glance at the tangled mass of wreckage and the crumpled figure in the road told them that, almost instantly. But the rear wheel of the motor-bicycle, which somehow had escaped damage, stuck up grotesquely in the air and still revolved slowly.

## CHAPTER X

Sometimes one sees in the Press complaint about the centralization of police affairs in too few hands. Those complaints are usually justifiable, but at the same time it is possible to produce arguments in favour of police methods by which every kind of event calling for police attention should be examined by the same central office. This could not be done, of course, without a system causing considerable inconvenience to individuals, as in Germany, where every citizen with any notable event in his life history has that history filed at police headquarters and continually brought up to date – an objectionable system in practice, as it happens, because of its necessary consequences of police dictatorialism, and 'personal papers,' and other encroachments upon individual liberty.

But in the particular case under review some such system

might have had its advantages. It is just possible that Morris's dossier at police headquarters (did such a system prevail in England) might have borne the endorsements that his departmental superior had been killed by an unknown hand, and that his departmental junior had been killed in a motor-bicycle accident immediately after leaving Morris's house. In that case official curiosity *might* have been aroused and an interesting inquiry initiated. Yet even then it is hardly likely that any correct deductions would be drawn.

As affairs actually turned out in Morris's case, nothing of the sort happened at all, as was only to be expected. Accidents to young men on motor-bicycles are far too common to cause much comment or inquiry, and the police officials who sorted out the facts regarding Reddy's death for the purposes of the inquest had nothing to do at all with those others who had already begun to shelve the mystery of Harrison's death as unsolvable.

It only called for a very stupid constable to collect the names and addresses of half a dozen drivers and other eye-witnesses of the event; and the discovery of the driving chain of Reddy's motor-bicycle high up on the hill was looked upon as the completion of the inquiry into the cause of the failure of the control of the machine, not as a very interesting first clue. Without his driving chain Reddy could not put the engine into bottom gear, and so use it as a brake, and with that point cleared up no one troubled to inquire very closely into why the two hand-brakes should have failed. A motor-bicycle which has collided with a tram, the one travelling at forty-five miles an hour, and the other at twenty, is sufficiently damaged for a couple of loose nuts not to be very remarkable. No breath of rumour came to the coroner (there was no rumour anywhere) as to anyone who would have found it to his interest to loosen those nuts; and it is rumour, with its concomitant anonymous letters, which usually provides a coroner with the initial line of thought on which to base an inquiry. Faulty motor-bicycle brakes are common enough, too. Morris was not even called upon to give evidence at the inquest, although he had been warned, in a routine fashion, that he might be called upon.

A coroner's jury heard a very rapid and perfunctory giving of evidence. They had read much in the newspapers regarding the unreliability of motor-bicycles, and they had frequently shaken their heads when helmeted young men had gone roaring past them with open exhausts. They had no hesitation at all in bringing in a verdict of accidental death, and in exonerating everyone concerned (except, by implication, the unfortunate victim) from all blame.

And that coroner's inquest was a counterpart of dozens of others being held all over the country. It meant next to nothing in the way of news to the newspapers, and consequently was hardly noticed in the Press; certainly not enough to attract the attention of the police who were dealing with Harrison's death; and, as has already been pointed out, it is extremely doubtful whether those police would have been interested, or would have made any correct deductions, had their attention been drawn to the coincidence. They would have been extremely clever men if they had read the scanty facts aright. Even a sorrowing father and a heartbroken mother had no suspicion at all, attributing the disaster to the natural failure of a machine which they had always regarded with a rather jealous and conservative dislike.

For that matter even people who knew Morris well (as well, that is to say, as a secret murderer can be known) had no suspicions, either; although they commented on the coincidence which had deprived the Universal Advertising Agency of two of its employees within ten days, they did so only with the same obviousness as they commented on the fact that the days were drawing in now. Mrs Morris had a splendid new event to discuss with the housewives in her street who were sweeping their steps when she set forth shopping. For a few days, until the novelty wore off, she enjoyed a delicious prestige as almost the last person to whom a man had spoken before meeting a violent death, and as the wife of a man who nearly had to give evidence at a coroner's inquest. But she had no ideas at all regarding the cause of the event. Nor did Mr Campbell, who, after commenting on the sad way in which a promising young man had met a sudden end, fell to discussing with Morris the replacing of him in the office without further thought. The incident, indeed, served to increase the growing esteem with which Mr Campbell regarded Morris, because Mr Campbell was very impressed by the keen and unfaltering manner in which Morris went through the list of applicants and selected the best from among them. Morris's choice of subordinates was sound, and he had at the moment no friends or relatives whom he wished to help into a job working under him. Maudie shed a sentimental tear or two over the fate of the fair-haired young man who had given her an occasional smile, but Reddy's shyness had made the smiles sufficiently rare for Maudie not to feel his loss too acutely.

There was only one person in the whole world who drew the correct conclusion, and that, naturally, was Oldroyd. He heard the news, as everyone else at the office did, on Monday morning; it was told him by a tearful Maudie. He received it stolidly; it was not until he heard the details of the loose nuts on the spring link of the driving chain, and of the faulty brakes, and of the fact that Reddy had just left Morris's house, that his suspicions began to form. Morris that morning at the office was in his most driving mood. He continually deplored the loss of this one of his three assistants and he piled work upon Oldroyd and Howlett in greater quantities even than usual; more even than was necessary, because, as he announced, he himself might have to be absent next day as witness at the inquest. Somehow Oldroyd could not help feeling a flicker of admiration for the fellow who could speak about the inquest so calmly, and who could meet Oldroyd's eye without a tremor.

Oldroyd sat at his table toiling over lay-outs, while his slow brain was fitting evidence together as neatly as his fingers were fitting together advertisements. He was not the sort of man to leap instantly to a conclusion; it took time to form one. Behind him sat Morris, firing out orders and decisions like shots from a gun, supervising four men's work, dictating letters to Maudie, and generally plunged into the rush of business which delighted him. When Oldroyd brought up completed bits of work to him, he looked them coldly over and discussed them side by side with Oldroyd as dispassionately as if there had never been any secret between them. It was his example, in fact, which enabled Oldroyd to get through that nightmare morning without giving way. Otherwise that matter-of-fact young man could never have tolerated the incongruity of working with a man who had the day before been guilty of a heartless murder.

Unremitting work brought a breathing space at length, and Morris sent Oldroyd out to lunch. Oldroyd was a man of healthy appetite; perhaps it would have taken more than the recent news to have rendered him incapable of eating, but it was sufficient to take away enough of his interest in food to order his lunch carelessly, with hardly a glance at the menu, and to eat it without noticing whether it was well or ill-cooked. And as his jaws slowly masticated the tough stewed steak his mind was slowly chewing over the facts it had gathered from Maudie's and Clarence's hurried account of the event of yesterday. By the time he had finished his meal he was convinced of Morris's guilt, and he was filled with a slow rage. His mind was not quick enough to have proceeded yet to the next stages of trying to work out how the occurrence would affect him personally, nor how, if he should wish to, he could avenge it. The only point he had reached so far was a hatred of the man who could send a boy to his death so heartlessly, and with so negative a motive. Oldroyd was fond of Reddy, but that was only a contributory factor to his anger. Mostly he was possessed with an angry loathing of the man who could plot and plan so cunningly, and who could carry out his plans so cold-heartedly. He had begun to regard Morris with the same shuddering antipathy as he would a snake; he felt that he could kill Morris as readily as he would kill a snake.

Then, walking back to the office along the crowded Strand, he saw Morris coming towards him. Instantly his rage came to a head. He hated the burly, insolent fellow with his bowler hat tilted at a jaunty angle, swaggering in his guilt among his fellow-creatures. Morris saw Oldroyd, nodded to him and prepared to pass him by, but Oldroyd stretched out a large hand and caught him by the breast of his coat; the two of them came to a sudden halt facing each other, causing a temporary congestion among the pedestrian traffic of the Strand. Morris looked down at Oldroyd with arrogant inquiry; Oldroyd glared up at Morris, dumb with rage.

'Well?' asked Morris superciliously.

'You killed that boy!' growled Oldroyd between his clenched teeth.

Oldroyd experienced a fierce sudden joy at seeing Morris wince and look apprehensively about him in case the muttered words should have caught the ear of any of the hurrying passers-by. But the roar of the traffic submerged the stifled articulation.

'You did!' said Oldroyd, drawing closer, with his right fist clenched and ready at his side.

But Morris had recovered himself instantly. His superb confidence in himself and in the strength of his position asserted itself at once.

'Come up here,' said Morris, turning towards a quieter by-street which led away from the Strand.

'Come on,' he repeated; 'don't make a fool of yourself here.'

That was the argument which had the most instant, most effective appeal. Oldroyd might be at grips with a murderer and involved in the most tangled meshes of crime, but he still could not contemplate making a scene in a public place. His English self-consciousness would not permit it the instant he was reminded of the possibility. His grip on Morris's coat relaxed, and he suffered himself to be led up the quiet street, where foot passengers were scarce enough to allow of a well-adjusted conversation not to be overheard. Then Morris turned and faced Oldroyd squarely, as squarely as he was meeting this new complication.

'What was it you were saying?' asked Morris.

'You heard well enough,' growled Oldroyd, the edge of his anger blunted by the tiny delay.

'Well, what were you going on to say after that?' asked Morris.

'I – I—' said Oldroyd. He had no idea at all what he was intending to say at that meeting in the Strand.

'I thought there wasn't much you could say,' sneered Morris. 'See here, young fellow, it'd be a lot better for you if you didn't interfere. Oh, I don't mean in *that* way' – Oldroyd had made a gesture of defiance – 'I'd fight you, and be glad of it, any time. But you'd better not go round making accusations like that.'

'Why not?' snarled Oldroyd.

'Because you can't do any good, and you might, you *might* do yourself a hell of a lot of harm. You can't prove what you said just now – and it's not true, anyway.'

These last words were added in a perfunctory manner; it is believed that Morris only said them to add an airy grace to his arrogant impregnableness.

'Chuck it,' said Oldroyd.

'Anyway, that's not the point at present. What I don't want you to forget is this; if you start thinking things like that, and trying to prove them, you'll get yourself into the hell of a mess. You might start people talking, you know. These things are the devil once rumours start going round. And people might start asking questions again about the *other thing* that happened. You know what I mean. And the case is just the same now as it ever was. Don't you ever forget that you're an accessory to that, you're as guilty as – as anyone else is. If you try to bring me down you'll bring yourself down, too. Mark that, I say. You'll find out what hanging's like if you start getting careless.'

Oldroyd was left wordless, staring up at the fleshy face and the bold, leering eyes. He was beside himself with baffled rage. He even stamped in his anger. Morris laughed at this exhibition. It was pleasing to his vanity to see this fellow balked and outwitted at every turn, and Oldroyd knew it and was further enraged by it.

'I'm not worrying,' spluttered Oldroyd. 'I'll get you yet, somehow, you devil!'

Morris laughed again; his vanity was having a rare feast today. He thought of another little dramatic touch he could add which pleased his sense of the theatrical. His expression hardened quite spontaneously, and he leaned forward and tapped Oldroyd on the chest.

'And mark this, too,' he said solemnly, his eyes glaring into Oldroyd's: 'don't play with fire. You know what's happened to two men who've got in my way. They didn't last long, did they? I'm dangerous; I'm a dangerous man. You don't want to end suddenly as well, do you? Then go steady. Mind what you're about.'

Morris turned on his heel so as not to spoil the dramatic effect by further argument, and strolled away, his hat cocked on one side and his step lighthearted, while Oldroyd could only gaze after him immobile.

For a little while the threat and the memory of those wild-beast eyes struck fear into Oldroyd. He knew now that he was afraid of the hulking fellow, afraid of his cunning and his craft, as well as repelled by the same kind of antipathy with which he would regard a reptile. But Oldroyd was a man of stout heart. He shook off his physical fear with a sturdy reliance on his own ability to keep himself out of harm's way; he even came to feel that Morris could not be very dangerous, seeing that he was incautious enough to utter that warning. By the time Oldroyd had reached the office he had come to the commonsense decisions to move cautiously, not to trust Morris in the least, and to keep his eyes open, watching an opportunity to rid himself of the burden of guilt and doubt which irked him so. And as Oldroyd climbed the stairs to the Universal Advertising Agency's office an idea occurred to him which he typically expressed in a phrase of two words.

'King's Evidence,' said Oldroyd to himself, mounting the stairs. 'By gum, that'd beat him! King's Evidence!'

It was a phrase which Oldroyd was to repeat to himself fairly often during the time to come. He found a vague comfort in it somehow. It was a last resource of safety; he thought of it as a sailorman on a lee shore thinks of his lifebelt. He was still murmuring 'King's Evidence' to himself as he reached the composing room, although he was not so bemused as not to check himself when he came into the presence of Clarence and Shepherd and Howlett. But he took no interest in the conversation which was engrossing them in Morris's absence. That was about a subject unpleasant to him. And he could feel a little amused at the guilty hurry with which they broke off their conversation and started hasty work the moment Morris came back into the room after the rapid lunch which was all that he allowed himself nowadays. It was amazing how much ascendancy Morris had acquired over those lads during his brief days of authority.

Morris entered briskly and sat himself at once at his table, reaching out automatically to the piles of papers heaped upon it. He had not allowed Oldroyd's little rebellion to interfere with his lunch, nor would he allow it to hinder his work. The only moral effect the incident had had upon him was to please his vanity, and to confirm him in his belief in the solidity of his position. Morris was vain, as criminals generally are; he was pleased with himself and his achievements. Although he was still clear enough in thought to have appreciated any serious weakness which might become apparent, it is to be doubted whether any minor weakness would have disturbed him at all. Two successful crimes had confirmed him in that feeling of certain immunity which distinguishes his kind, and which will frequently support them to the very steps of the scaffold. Not the least thought of the scaffold crossed Morris's mind, and he dismissed Oldroyd's show of opposition with contempt from his consideration. Also his feeling of the dignity of his position in the office helped him not to confuse Oldroyd the slow, reliable, thoughtful clerk, with Oldroyd the asscessory before the fact and the source of possible danger. He made the fullest use of the services of Oldroyd the clerk.

## CHAPTER XI

It is very difficult after the event to reconstuct the character of a criminal. The people one consults who came into contact with him are biased one way or the other, and they like to believe in their own perspicacity. One man will say, 'It was obvious from his expression,' and another will tell you that 'he was a plausible scoundrel, very plausible. He would have taken almost anybody in, but he didn't deceive me. There was something about him – something not quite trustworthy. It might have been in the way he looked at you, or the way he spoke. I had my doubts about him from the very first.' And another, more honest, will say, 'I don't believe he was guilty at all. He was always very nice to me.'

So that the truth is hard to come by. As far as Mrs Morris is concerned, it is to be believed that she never had any suspicion of her husband until the end, even if she did then. But, then, Mrs Morris loved her husband in a queer cross-grained way; moreover, the changes which might have been observable in Morris were mere accentuations of his outstanding characteristics, and could have been attributed quite plausibly to other factors, such as his promotion in the office. He used to come home more tired, for instance – exhausted would be a better word, perhaps. But, then, he was working harder. He was surer of himself, he carried himself with more dignity, he was vainer – but that could be readily explained by his responsible position in the Universal Advertising Agency. He may have been a trace more irritable, less tolerant of the noises his children made, but that was not a very noticeable difference from what he had been before. He was undoubtedly more taciturn towards his wife, but she, poor woman, was more likely to attribute that to a natural waning of his affection for her than to the fact that he had committed a crime.

Morris, indeed, began to treat his wife with a lofty indifference which was only slightly paralleled by his previous behaviour. His idea of his own importance was inflating daily;

partly this was because of the ambitious dreams which he was dreaming, partly it was a result of his late marvellous successes, and partly because he had had to take more interest than usual in the significance of his own actions and demeanour, and consequently bulked larger in his own world than he had done before. His belief and pride in himself, indeed, began to approach in degree the enormous egoism of a lunatic; other people to him were beginning to appear as insignificant as ants; they were mere tools and instruments which he could use and throw aside. The main characteristic of a criminal, the *sine qua non* in any definition, is an unusual idea of the importance of his own well-being compared with the importance of the well-being, or the opinions, or the ideals of other people. Morris would not have killed Harrison had he not thought Harrison's life of less importance than his own happiness, and had he not been supported by his belief in his own skill in avoiding detection.

So that the egoism, the superior idea of himself, was well established already, and later development inevitably tended to increase it inordinately. He began to regard his wife with no more concern than he did any other article of furniture in his home. He came home that Monday night and sat by the fire without a word to her. Molly came to his side and began her usual tiresome attempts to interest him in her own trivial self, but Morris was able to ignore her so completely that she soon gave up. Mary Morris, ironing the day's washing, addressed her usual insignificant remarks to him, and received in answer unintelligible monosyllables.

'You might answer when you're spoken to,' she said sharply.

'M'm,' said Morris. That was a purely reflex action, a legacy from the days when he had been accustomed to speaking to her.

'Did you hear what I said?' she demanded, changing the irons with a clatter.

'M'm,' said Morris.

Mrs Morris set down the hot iron on the stand and put her hand on her hip.

'Charlie!' she said. 'Charlie, why don't you speak when you're spoken to? Charlie!'

There seemed some possibility here of a lively conversation.

'M'm,' said Morris, lighting a second cigarette.

Mrs Morris stared at him.

'Aren't you well?' she demanded, and then, thinking to touch his heart, 'Don't you want your supper?'

'M'm,' said Morris.

Mrs Morris sighed hopelessly. There was no possibility of conversation or argument while he was in this mood. She finished her ironing in a silence broken only by the thump of the iron on the table. Morris was quite unaware that she had spoken to him at all. He was above all that. Mrs Morris cleared away the ironing blanket and took Molly off to bed with no further word. She came down again and laid the supper.

'It's ready,' she said, and Morris's egoism permitted him to hear that.

He pulled up a chair to the table and took up the carving knife and fork. The nice leg of mutton which had been so glorious a spectacle yesterday was still comparatively well-looking. He cut himself some beautiful thick slices and ate them with quantitites of bread and butter, drinking two cups of strong tea the while. The plateful finished, he eyed the joint. It was good mutton, this. Mechanically he took up the carving knife and fork again.

'Oh, Charlie,' said Mary reproachfully, 'there's our dinner tomorrow to come off that.'

Morris looked round at her expressionlessly and, without a word turned back again to the dish and continued to pile his plate again. Perhaps his own conception of his own sublime importance may have penetrated to Mrs Morris's mind; at any rate, she gave up all attempt at hindering and dutifully refilled his cup when he clattered it imperiously in its saucer.

Plenty of mutton, cut thick, and with its due allowance of fat, bolted ravenously along with three large cups of strong tea, might be expected to trouble the stomach of a superman. Certainly it began to irritate the digestion of Mr Morris. He was not conscious of indigestion. A really sharp stomach ache or the depression accompanying dyspepsia might conceivably have brought Mr Morris down from the rosy clouds in which he was drifting. But Mr Morris's internal apparatus was of too stout stuff to yield so entirely to maltreatment. It stuck to its guns and tackled the heavy task of digesting the indigestible with quite a fair measure of success. All that troubled Mr Morris's soul was a vague feeling of unrest, a mild irritability, certainly not sufficiently to disquiet him. Subconsciously he may have felt that, remarkably, there was something wanting in his astonishingly complete universe. He went to no particular trouble to analyse the subject further. Old-established reflex habits asserted themselves.

One important item in Morris's ideal of a fleshly paradise was the presence of women; women not particularly for ornament, but for use. Seeing that he felt something missing from his present paradise, and seeing that no woman was included therein at the moment, his subconscious self came to the natural conclusion that what he wanted was a woman; it was a conclusion which accorded well with old habits of thought and action. Mary was at hand, and Mary's lack of novelty was no real demerit. He was so far above all other humans that the differences between other individuals were insignificant to him. As Mary passed by his chair when she came in again from the scullery after washing up he reached out a heavy hand and seized hold of her.

'Oh, Charlie,' said Mrs Morris, 'I've got an awful lot to do, you know.'

But there was a tone in her voice which went to show that his heavy-handed attention was not displeasing to her – not that Morris would have cared if it were.

'Oh, Charlie,' said Mrs Morris; she almost giggled, though, for all that.

He dragged her across to him and pulled her down heavily on to his knee. Mrs Morris had always loved his big thick arms and burly shoulders. He crushed her down to him and pressed rough kisses upon her, and she offered no objection. She was a self-assertive little person, and she had a good opinion of herself whenever housekeeping cares left her time to think about it; but all the same she was secretly rather pleased by a strong-handed wooing, preceded as it was by an interval of neglect which had allowed an opportunity for her to lose a little of her self-assurance, and for Morris to rise correspondingly in her esteem. The very roughness of his coat was grateful to her, somehow, and when there came a lull in Morris's brutal caresses (a result of a vague realization that the present situation was not calculated, after all, to relieve his mild irritability) she snuggled up to him closer still.

'Charlie,' she whispered in the little hoarse voice which Charlie remembered of old – he had heard it before in the dark evenings of their early wooing. That association of ideas and Mary's eager little caresses had their usual effect upon him. He turned to her again and his arms tightened about her. He kissed her brutally; he wooed her, as ever, as gluttonously as he ate.

But the trivial diversions of a superman have no special interest for us. There is no particular appeal for us even in the picture of Morris in bed that night, sleeping heavily and noisily with his mouth half open, the muddled bedclothes piled upon him, and his thick coarse hair in a black tangle upon the white pillow. That does not make at all an alluring picture; Charlie Morris was not at all an alluring character. But the picture at least shows him enjoying a sleep deep enough and untroubled enough to be envied by many. He was passing a night far happier and far more comfortable than the one, for instance, which he had spent immediately before entering upon his career of crimes of violence.

Some may explain it one way, and some may explain it another. One authority might attribute it to relief from financial anxiety; another, more subtle and more cynical, might lay it down that the crimes Morris had committed were a comfort to him, a fulfilment of his suppressed desires. And some might say that Morris was merely a stolid conscienceless brute with neither feelings nor aspirations. Those that read to the end of this book may better take their choice of these conflicting opinions.

## CHAPTER XII

The affairs of the Universal Advertising Agency were looking up; there was no doubt about it. Twice in one week had elegant Mr Lewis come hastening into the office, his baby eyes wide with excitement, to tell the glad news of a new account which was to be entrusted to them. The sale of Ultra-violet Soap had expanded so much, either because of or in spite of the work of the Agency, that the proprietors, like sensible men, had decided to increase their advertising appropriation, and with it, in consequence, the Agency's commission. It was only six weeks after his last rise in salary that Mr Morris was told by

Mr Campbell that he was to receive another one – his income rose now to the colossal height of six pounds ten a week; and the whole office was delighted to hear of the distribution of a fortnight's pay among them as a Christmas bonus.

Mr Morris was a good advertising man. He had the directness of vision which enabled him to see that the object of advertising was to sell; consequently he was trammelled by none of the ideals which might have hindered a better educated man. To him an advertisement could only be beautiful or well worded if it was likely to promote sales; it involved a contradiction in terms to speak of a well-worded advertisement which did not do so. Split infinitives and 'different to's' meant nothing to him as long as they did not detract from the appeal of the advertisement to the class of person to whom it was addressed. He was never likely in consequence to lose time in struggling towards an unattainable but delicious ideal of beauty; certainly he would never be responsible for the production of an admirable drawing or an exquisite piece of prose which left the reader quite charmed but without the least urge to buy the product advertised. Vulgarity meant nothing unpleasant to him if vulgarity achieved its end. Arguments might even be put forward, therefore, to show that Morris was an idealist in his way, although his ideals were not those of an artistic minority.

Certainly Mr Campbell, shrewd but lacking in vigour, well appreciating the object of advertising but shrinking fastidiously from the means necessary to attain it, found that Morris saved him a great deal of trouble and earned him a great deal of money. The propositions Morris brought forward were so obviously promising that he could not fail to see their efficacy, and Morris couuld urge their adoption so earnestly that Mr Campbell could sigh and grant it without a feeling of personal responsibility for the new burst of inartistic vulgarity which was to be inflicted on the world. As Morris declared triumphantly, and as Mr Campbell admitted with whimsical sorrow, the people who looked for taste in drawings or correctness of English in an advertisement usually had not the money or not the faintest inclination to buy Ultra-violet Soap or Sleepwell Beds, and Morris saw no object whatever in throwing away the good seed of labour and money upon the stony ground of their poverty or indifference. He worked upon the taste and superstition of the massed majority, the housewives doing their Friday shopping and the men at Saturday football matches, and they in return spent their pennies and sixpences as he vociferously directed them.

There was no doubt about that at all. The work the Universal Advertising Agency was doing was beginning to be talked about among the men with advertising appropriations to spend; business was coming its way rapidly.

'We shall have to be increasing our staff before long at this rate,' said Mr Campbell to Morris, à propos of nothing in particular.

'Yes, I can see it coming,' said Morris.

Mr Campbell tapped at his desk with the end of his pencil and looked across at Morris somewhat nervously.

'I could bring you a new clerk next week, if you like,' he said.

'There's work enough for another one,' replied Morris. He was choosing his words carefully, for he realized that Mr Campbell did not approach a proposition thus indirectly without good cause.

'Quite untrained,' said Mr Campbell. 'I suppose you could teach the elements of lay-out and sizes of type and things like that?'

Morris's face fell a little; he did not want to do anything of the kind, but Mr Campbell clearly wished it, and his position was not yet strong enough by any means to counter Mr Campbell's wishes directly.

'I could do with a good lay-out man, or a copy writer—' he began doubtfully, but Mr Campbell interrupted.

'This won't be a lay-out *man*,' he said. 'I was thinking about my daughter.'

'Oh!' said Morris.

'You've seen her, I expect.' Morris certainly could remember a shingled, well-dressed girl in her late teens who sometimes came to call for Mr Campbell at his office. 'She's nearly grown up by now. I thought a year or two in this office might do her a bit of good.'

'It might,' said Morris.

'All girls ought to work for their livings for a time, I think,' went on Mr Campbell. 'But I can't think of anyone who would be likely to employ my daughter if I don't.'

He said it in the deprecating fashion of a proud parent.

'Oh, that'll be all right, of course,' said Morris.

87

'I'm glad you think so. She will be working in your room just like the others, of course. I don't want to do it unless you are sure that it won't upset things.'

'Oh, no, of course it won't,' said Morris, who did not feel nearly as sure about it as he tried to appear. The presence of a girl of that sort would mean a mincing attention to what one said, and to the similes one employed, and would be an infernal nuisance all round; but one does not raise unreasonable objections of that sort to an idea which is clearly near to one's employer's heart.

'Right,' said Mr Campbell. 'She'll come in next Monday, then, and start a first-hand study of what the great world is really like.' And next Monday, as good as his word, Mr Campbell appeared at the composing-room door with his hand on his daughter's shoulder.

'Here we are then, Mr Morris,' he said. 'Here's your new assistant. Keep her up to scratch, mind. There, Doris, I suppose that's your chair and table. Mr Morris will start you off on your duties. Be a good girl.'

An ordinarily unobservant individual might have said that he saw dozens of girls exactly like Doris Campbell every day in the street. She was just of that type, taller than the average of the preceding generation, slim and trim and shingled, well dressed, apparently self-assured, clearly a good dancer and a good tennis player, but with nothing else to distinguish her from all her fellow nineteen-year-olds in her class of society.

No one in the composing room paid her any special attention at first; everyone there had greeted the news of her approaching arrival amongst them with groans and grumblings, and perhaps for as much as two days after it they would not have recognized her had they passed her in the street.

Then she began to differentiate herself from the mass of the outer world, just as any girl will if one sees enough of her. Soon everyone in the composing room could have said for certain that she had grey eyes and black hair; if they could not have stated with precision the prevailing colour of her office jumper, they would at least take notice when she wore a different one. Young Shepherd became her attentive slave; elegant young Lewis, the outside man, found frequent occasion to explain subtle points of advertising to her at her table beside Morris's dais. She soon recovered from the agonizing shyness and the dazed sense of uselessness which oppressed her when

88

she first came, and was able to look the young men in the face with her steady grey eyes. Living in that atmosphere no one could possibly avoid picking up the jargon of the profession. Soon she was able to talk about fourteen point type and six-inch double columns with the best of them. Mr Campbell, watching anxiously to see the effect of an experiment he had not been too sure about, was overjoyed. Possibly the only people who thoroughly disliked the presence of the new arrival were the typists, whose hats and stockings and shoes, trim and neat though they might be, could never compete with those of a girl who was the only daughter of a man whose large income was steadily increasing.

Her presence had a very marked effect on Mr Morris. As her instructor he had necessarily most to do with her. Whenever he could spare time from all the manifold work he had to do, he would sit at a second chair at Miss Campbell's table and explain to her the elements of the art.

'It's easy enough, Miss Campbell. Look here, these blokes, the Elsinore Cork Company, want some new ads. got out. You get hold of the file with what we've said about 'em before. That's Shepherd's job to find it out for you. Of course, they only advertise in the technical press. No one except cold storage people and so on want to buy compressed cork. Here's a booklet about their stuff, for instance. If you look through that you soon see what they're proud of. It's light, and it's cheap, and it won't warp, and you can stick it on to anything with any kind of glue. Right. You want to get all that into one ad. and sing a whole song about one of those points. So you start off with big type. "Save weight!" Something like that to catch the eye of the man turning over the advertisement pages. Then you've got to explain that: "Elsinore Compressed Cork weighs less per square foot than any other on the market." It doesn't matter much if it doesn't. If someone kicks up a fuss it's easy to find some particular case where you're right. But you have to rub it in. Just saying that doesn't fix it in a chap's mind. You've got to have a drawing of a workman carrying great slabs of the stuff on the back of his neck, or something, and smiling all over his face at the easiness of it. *Then*, when you've made your big point, you can go on and make the others. "And it's cheaper than other brands, too, and you can't make it warp if you try; and as for sticking! – any quick-drying glue will stick it for you in no time." That makes a good ad.

And then the week after you make the next point the big one. "Cut your replacement costs!" and the next week, "Do your cork slabs do this or that"; and the week after, "You can't pry it loose with a crowbar!" You don't have to know anything special about the stuff to advertise it. All you have to remember is to say the main thing three times over – in big type, and then in a drawing, and then in little type. That's a good ad., then, of the easy kind. Wonderful how it lasts. It'll work over and over again in that kind of paper.'

'You make it sound awfully easy,' said Miss Campbell, gazing fascinated at Morris's thick hands flipping over the filed advertisements and producing example after example to prove his points unhesitatingly.

'Oh, don't you run away with the idea that it's as easy as all that,' said Morris. 'Any fool can make up some kind of ad. Lots of fools try. But it isn't a fool who can make up a *good* ad. You've got to use just the right word and have the type just the right size, and you've got to see that the artist gets just your idea into his drawing. Clarence, over there, always wants to put his own ideas in, and those damned – dashed, I mean – those dashed studios always do the same, too, if they have any ideas at all. You can't have that at all. These artistic blokes always think they know best, and they don't. You take that from me, Miss Campbell – they don't. They never do. There never was an artist yet who could make up a good ad. – an ad. worth calling an ad. I don't expect Einstein – is it Einstein or Epstein? – anyway, you know the bloke I mean – ever had an idea for an ad. that we'd give tuppence for. I'm sure of it. If he had, I don't expect he'd stay an artist long.'

'I don't expect he would,' said Miss Campbell, and felt very pleased with herself on account of this secretly witty remark, while Morris rubbed his chin and grinned down at her in huge satisfaction at being able to spread himself thus.

Morris never found himself regretting for a moment Mr Campbell's decision to bring his daughter to the office. She brought a new interest into the composing room. It was the first time he had come into contact with a girl of her class. That apparent assurance of manner even at the shyest moment, that obviously well-bred voice were things he had long envied – and sneered at to his friends who did not possess them. Certainly they were in remarkable contrast with his wife's manners; even Maudie appeared now to his newly meticulous taste to be flamboyant and badly dressed. Anyway, he had found out long ago, by experiment, that Maudie was easy of approach, whereas Miss Campbell was unattainable. It was some time before Morris progressed beyond this realization. He was long satisfied with peacocking in front of her, with admiring her daintiness from afar; he found absurd pleasure in her proximity when they sat side by side studying advertising. It was only gradually that he began to form the sneaking ambition to attain the unattainable; and before he really did so affairs between him and Oldroyd had reached a crisis.

Lamb and Howlett were new to the office; Clarence cared little about anyone there; Shepherd noticed nothing ominous in the atmosphere, because his attention was entirely filled up by Morris's insistence on his doing all the work he could cram into his time, and by his new devotion to Miss Campbell, and by all the pleasurable excitement of the successful development of the office. Only Oldroyd was conscious of the horror of the situation. He alone knew that what the Press would have delighted to call a 'human tiger' was stalking about the office. Sturdily unimaginative as he was, he still found himself at times indulging in the wildest mental imagery; he would realize with a shock that he had been looking at Morris's thick lips and telling himself that they had tasted blood. Morris could hardly smile without Oldroyd quoting to himself a half-forgotten line of Shakespeare: 'A man may smile and smile and smile and be a villain.' His loathing of the man increased day by day; he was filled with a shuddering fear of the fellow who could grin amicably one day and kill the next.

He found himself at times wondering who would be Morris's next victim, wondering who there was who stood now in his way; and often he came to the sickly conclusion that it was he, Oldroyd, from whom Morris had most to fear, and who might, therefore, be the object of Morris's Satanic wrath. But, though he knew himself afraid, Oldroyd still had enough sturdy courage to stay where he was and endure the troubles Fate and his own weakness had brought upon him. He set his teeth and refused to admit the possibility of Morris's gaining an ascendancy over him. But it was very bad for his work.

One bright morning the fact was thrust upon him. The while he was racking his tired brain for ideas for a new layout Miss Campbell went off with her father for lunch; Shepherd was out on an errand, and then Morris sent Clarence and Lamb and Howlett out together to their lunches as well. Something in Morris's cold, flat voice told Oldroyd that there was danger in the air; he could tell now when Morris was posing – but he could never tell whether Morris was merely planning a murder or some scheme for smartening up the staff. When the footsteps of the trio had died away outside the door Oldroyd heard Morris address him across the room.

'Oldroyd,' said Morris, 'come here a minute.'

There was a menace in his voice; Oldroyd knew the fellow too well by now. All the same, Oldroyd heaved himself out of his chair and shambled across to the dais. He felt he hated a world which put him under the orders of Morris.

'Now look here, Oldroyd,' began Morris judicially, 'you know what I want to speak about.'

'No, that I don't,' was the sullen reply.

'I think you do. I sent those others out so that I wouldn't have to tell you off in front of them. You're not doing the least dam' bit of good in this office.'

'Oh, aren't I?' said Oldroyd. He was inclined to snarl a little, such was his mood of angry mutiny.

'I'm warning you,' said Morris – and anyone could have guessed that from the tone of his voice.

'There isn't a day goes by but someone has to clear up mistakes after you. You haven't made a decent suggestion for weeks. You're slow and you're careless and you're setting a bad example to the others. I can't have it in my office, Oldroyd, I tell you that; and, what's more, I'm not going to have it.'

'You aren't, aren't you?' said Oldroyd; he was not a man of repartee, but the tone of his voice implied most of the biting things he would have liked to say had he thought of them. He could not bring himself to knuckle under to Morris.

Morris's face had assumed a pained expression. It hurt his fine feelings that a junior employee should thus carry himself with a rebellious bearing towards a senior. He set an edge on his voice.

'That's enough of that,' he said. 'I'm warning you for your own good. If there isn't a big improvement soon I shall have to tell Mac that you're no use in this office. And that means that you go – quick, too. We'll give you a character all right – don't care who you work for as long as you don't work for us – but you'll go out of here.'

92

He looked across his desk at Oldroyd. His expression was calm; for that matter so were his feelings. There was nothing in this business of chiding a junior to ruffle a man like him. He eyed the struggle on Oldroyd's face quite dispassionately.

For Oldroyd was in a state of boiling fury – fury at his own impotence as much as at the insolent overbearingness of this man whom he knew so much about, and so uselessly. His features worked with the conflict of his emotions. The yearning to say something effective, the ingrained caution resulting from years of employment which warned him to do nothing to offend his employer, his fear and his fury with himself for his fear, all these combined into a very explosive mixture in Oldroyd's soul. The internal pressure rose until two words were forced out of Oldroyd's mouth; he hardly knew he had said them.

'King's Evidence!' said Oldroyd hoarsely, glaring back at Morris's stony stare.

Oldroyd felt a fierce joy at seeing the effect of his words. Morris's expression lost some of its impersonal quality, and he leaned a little forward towards Oldroyd across the table.

'What's that you said?' he demanded sharply.

'I said, "King's Evidence!" Do you hear me? King's Evidence!'

Morris had recovered control over himself almost instantly.

'I don't understand,' he said coldly.

'Oh, don't you? Well, you soon will. I've been thinking things over' – Oldroyd had at any rate not been thinking the things he was saying at present; they were the result of immediate inspiration – 'I've been thinking, I tell you. You just try and sack me from here and see what I do then, that's all. What d'you think the police will say if I go to them and say I can tell them about—'

He was checked by Morris's frantic gesticulations for silence. Morris scrambled out of his chair and down from the dais and hurried in absurd haste to the door to make certain they were not being overheard. When he came back Oldroyd was calmer, because he was far more confident.

'Yes,' went on Oldroyd, 'King's Evidence. You know what that means. If they can hang *you* on what *I* can prove they won't hang *me*. They'd like to know how Harrison died, wouldn't they? *And Reddy, too?* You sack me, you put me out of a job, and that's what they'll do. So there!'

Oldroyd glared defiantly at Morris, who had come up close to him, and stood towering over him, hands clasping and unclasping. Morris's expression was one of dreadful rage. He would have been furious, in his new-found character of successful business man, at defiance from an inferior in any case. But this – this mad threat, this wild assault on his unassailable position, this pitting by Oldroyd of his little wits and determination against Morris's vast brain and superhuman personality, nearly drove Morris frantic. The wound to his pride was enormous. And he saw the danger. If Oldroyd were, as Morris had threatened, dismissed from the employ of the Universal Advertising Agency, he might easily be desperate enough to carry out his threat. Even if the police did not advise accepting Oldroyd as King's Evidence, they might be set on the right track by his plea, so that Morris as well as Oldroyd would go to the gallows. Even if Oldroyd saw this possibility he might not be deterred in his present state of blind fury, or in the cold desperation into which dismissal would plunge him. Morris suddenly found himself helpless. It was maddening to find himself, the clever, cunning, amazingly skilful Morris, at the mercy of this little fellow with the silly little moustache. It was just as maddening, oddly enough, for Morris, as a man of vast designs in the advertising world, to be defied by a little whippersnapper of a clerk.

For a space the brute in Morris seemed likely to assume control over the proceedings. Morris found himself drawing himself together, bunching himself up for a spring upon Oldroyd. His eyes were already seeking out the spot on his neck where his big hands would take their grip. His fingers were growing rigid and bent, like talons. Oldroyd noticed the menace in Morris's attitude – he could hardly have failed to do so – and he in turn began to crouch forward to receive the spring; his lips went back a little from his teeth and he braced himself to fight for his life.

But even as the two men edged closer together Morris's plotting brain set a check on his bad temper. It would never do for him to indulge in an unseemly scuffle with a junior in the very heart of the office. The desire to rend and tear Oldroyd, to leave him a crumpled wreck on the floor was still present, but it was held back by his caution. And were he to kill Oldroyd there and then – and Oldroyd had been near to death at one moment – it would not be a neat murder, without trace.

Morris would have to bear the consequences of it. Lastly his enormous vanity came to his rescue in a contrary kind of way. He would not mind yielding to the fellow's demands, appearing to give way, because he was perfectly certain of over-reaching him in the end. Oldroyd might score a point, but Morris had already scored so many that he need not mind. He could leave Oldroyd his thousands as long as he himself had his tens of thousands.

And, having once made up his mind in this fashion, his natural scheming self carried the notion through without difficulty, without further thought. His muscles relaxed, his shoulders straightened up out of their menacing crouch. His thick lips assumed the smile of coarse geniality which sat so commonly upon them.

'All right,' he said. 'You've done me this time. I don't see how I can buck against you as long as you're set on making a fool of yourself. I've got to put up with you, I suppose.'

Oldroyd backed warily away from him before he, too, discarded his defensive attitude.

'All right,' he said hoarsely. His mouth and throat were parched with excitement.

'You can do what you like in this damned office, I suppose, now,' said Morris. He spoke in a tone full of the bitterness of defeat – just the tone which might be expected of him. Yet he knew none of that bitterness; his voice took on that tone instinctively, for Morris was a plotter born.

'Yes,' replied Oldroyd. He was still suspicious; no one knowing as much about Morris as he did would be otherwise.

'But look here, old man,' said Morris pleadingly, 'don't come it over me too much. The others'll guess that something's up if you do. Do a bit of work now and then, there's a good chap. We can't afford to take chances, either of us.'

His plotter's instinct told him that the best tactics at the moment were to lure his enemy into a state of over-confidence, and his every word and gesture adapted themselves at once to this end. His own perfect confidence in his ability to crush Oldroyd enabled him to humble himself thus without any wound to his self-esteem.

'I'll see,' said Oldroyd cautiously.

'I'll tell you what!' exclaimed Morris. 'Let's try working together. We've never done it yet. Why, you and I, Oldroyd – you with your brains and me being so pally with Campbell –

we might do anything. Let's back each other up. This office is going to be a big thing one of these days, you know.'

There was absolutely nothing jarring in the pose or in the accent as Morris uttered the honeyed words. But as he said them there fluttered across Oldroyd's mind a pictured memory of another scene in that same room – of Reddy being brought to shake hands with Morris and with him, the very day before Reddy was sent to his death. It was that memory which prevented Morris's pretty little speech from having the slightest effect upon Oldroyd. Yet all the same Oldroyd had learned something by now of intrigue from the master of intrigue who stood before him.

'All right, if you want to,' he said simply.

'Done!' said Morris, smiting his hand with his fist. 'That's fine! We'll be partners from now on. Why we'll—'

But Oldroyd was deprived of the felicity of hearing any more of the inventions of Mr Morris's ingenious mind by the entry of Miss Campbell, newly returned from lunch. She saw nothing at all unusual in Mr Morris's speaking vehemently to one of the staff and driving his points home with his fist on his hand. That was quite usual behaviour for Mr Morris.

'So you're back?' said Morris to Miss Campbell. That was the sort of speech to be expected of Mr Morris, whose small talk bore none of the indications of an original mind.

'I am,' said Miss Campbell, sitting down at her table and hunting for the cherished drawing which lay there half finished.

'Right!' said Morris. 'Then I can leave the office in good hands while I go and get my lunch. You'll see that nobody comes and pinches the furniture, won't you?'

He reached for his hat and coat and sauntered out of the room, remembering, all the same, to throw a glance of reminiscent friendliness in Oldroyd's direction. Certainly not Miss Campbell, probably no one at all, could have guessed that the room he left had just been the scene of a wild quarrel, and had nearly witnessed a struggle of life and death. In the same way, no one in the crowded Strand guessed that the thickset, jaunty young man with the fleshy features had two murders on his soul; certainly no one would possibly imagine that he was planning to rid himself of another possible enemy by the same abhorred crime.

# CHAPTER XIII

Morris's thoughts on the journey homeward that evening dwelt naturally on the subject of Oldroyd. There was no denying that the latter constituted a dangerous menace to Morris's happiness on more than one account. Morris's haughty vanity was touched by the thought that under him he had an employee whom he could not dare to dismiss and this, it may well be, was the mainspring of the emotion he felt. But besides that he was genuinely dissatisfied with the quality of Oldroyd's work, and he would gladly see him out of the office, which was rapidly gaining a distinguished place in Morris's affections and ambition. Lastly (and, let it be granted, leastly) came the fact that Morris was dependent for his life on Oldroyd's silence. That in itself was sufficient justification for the murder of Oldroyd, according to the simple moral standard which Morris maintained. But, in face of Oldroyd's capacity for harm, Morris refused to be frightened by it. It might affect his actions, but it did not cause him to feel afraid. Morris could not bring himself to believe that so obviously unimportant an individual as Oldroyd could be a danger to such a brilliant, successful, dangerous, clever person as Morris.

The main characteristic of the crime of which Morris was guilty is its tendency to reproduce itself. A second murder will incur no additional penalty if the first is to be discovered, so that fear of punishment does not act as a deterrent. Fear of discovery is very largely overridden by the knowledge of previous success, and any natural repugnance the criminal may feel towards the taking of human life is largely blunted by the time he begins to consider the repetition of the crime. So that Morris, coming home, was coolly planning the murder of Oldroyd, as dispassionately as a butcher might meditate the slaughter of a sheep.

'Coolly' and 'dispassionately' are misleading words in this connection, however. Morris fired with the zeal of plotting was a different man from Morris studying a restaurant menu, or even from Morris devising an advertisement. His pulse-rate rose, and his blood coursed more freely, and his brain worked more rapidly and more clearly. It seemed as if he could catch and seize inspiration out of the stream of unpromising data which he passed rapidly in review before his mind.

But it was a very, very difficult piece of constructive work to which Morris had applied himself. It is only when one is favoured with exceptional good fortune or unusual facilities that it is possible to kill a man in the heart of civilization without being found out. Morris came out of the station, he crossed the main road at the corner where Reddy met his death, and he walked up the steep hill – too fast, as usual – all the way to his house without having gained any inspiration from his creative mood. He felt balked and thwarted and annoyed by the time he had reached his front door.

The sitting-room was littered with toys and unmended clothes and all the other things to be expected in the sole living-room of a small house containing two children, just before those children's bedtime. Mrs Morris was sitting by the fire with John on her knee and John was howling most dolorously.

'Oh, my God!' said Morris, voicing his discontent with the world in general as much as his disgust with the sights that met his eyes and the noise that assailed his ears.

'Oh, don't you start, too!' snapped his wife. 'These kids have been enough to wear me out all day long.'

'Take him up to bed, then,' said Morris. 'It's past his bedtime, anyway.'

For once Mrs Morris was ready to act on a suggestion of her husband's. She rose from the chair with John in her arms, and John, with bedtime so near, and with everything in consequence to gain and nothing to lose, redoubled his howls and, writhing wildly in his mother's arms, beat the air impotently with his kicking feet. The piercing quality of his shrieks maddened Morris.

'Stop that, you little devil, can't you?' he demanded. 'Stop it!'

He took a stride towards the child, ready to strike; in justice to him it may be said at once that he most probably would have opened the clenched fist with which he menaced him before he struck. Mrs Morris gave a little cry and whirled round so as to interpose herself between her husband and her child. John was startled into two seconds' silence, but then, finding

98

himself safe behind his mother's shoulder, he began to howl once more. Morris uttered a fierce oath.

'Charlie!' said Mrs Morris, inexpressibly shocked. 'Not before the children!'

'Then take them away!' raved Morris. 'Oh, God lumme, take 'em away!'

He stamped his feet and clenched his fists, and Mrs Morris, thoroughly frightened, hastened out of the room, staggering under the weight of the big, heavy boy. John's howls dwindled in volume behind the closed door, and died away still more as Mrs Morris dragged his writhing form up the stairs. Morris made a disgusted noise in his throat and threw himself into his chair. Molly, as ever during these commotions, continued to play imperturbably on the hearthrug. The two of them were still in the same relative positions when Mrs Morris came back into the room after putting John to bed.

'I'll be dam' glad,' announced Morris, 'when these two kids have grown up a bit and stop being such an infernal worry.'

He glowered at his wife as he spoke, and by doing so he caught sight of a curious change in her expression. She opened her mouth to speak, but as she did so her glance wavered across to Molly on the hearthrug, and she shut it again. Obviously she trembled on the brink of speech for half a minute, and obviously she drew back again timorously.

'And what the hell's the matter with *you?*' demanded Morris crossly.

'Oh, nothing, nothing,' said his wife, but it was not the truth that she spoke; even Morris could see that.

It was not until much later, after Molly had been put to bed and Morris had eaten his supper, that Mary Morris began the subject which was so clearly distasteful to her; she dreaded the effect of her news on her husband and she bowed her head over her mending as she spoke, as much to prevent herself from seeing his expression as for concealing her own.

'You spoke about the kids growing up just now, Charlie,' said Mrs Morris.

'Well?'

'Well, you'll have to wait a bit longer, after all; there's another one coming.'

'Oh, my God!' said Morris.

The arrival of the two children of whom he was already the father had thoroughly robbed him of any paternal feelings he may have once had. He could picture far too clearly the course of approaching events. Mary would grow more and more helpless as the months went on. She would come to ask his aid in the domestic work of the house. It would be he who would have to carry the kids up to bed; there would be evenings when he would come home and find Mary lying down and he would have to cook his own supper; perhaps the scullery would even be piled high with the accumulation of a whole day's washing-up, which he would be expected to dispose of.

All that irked him inexpressibly. It would have gone against the grain long ago, when he would have resented the incongruity of a big, brawny man like himself having to do housework; now that his opinion of himself was far more exalted he hated the idea more violently than ever.

And his thoughts went on beyond that, too. There would be the time of the birth, when there would be a dictatorial nurse in the house. In his heart of hearts he knew (and was infuriated in consequence) that even he, the great Charlie Morris, would flinch and quail before that nurse and do her bidding humbly. Not merely that, but it would cost money – money for this and money for that, money for all sorts of unexpected items which it would be impossible either to foresee or to refuse. Morris was not a miser; he liked spending money freely, but he only liked spending money on himself. To spend it on a wailing baby whose arrival he positively did not desire was simply maddening. Years of penury had made Morris very sharp about obtaining full value for the money he disbursed.

Lastly, after the nurse had departed and matters had come back again nearly to their poor normal, there would still be trouble. The kid would wail in the night with that maddening persistence typical of kids. He would wail and wail, and Charlie Morris knew by experience that not even the great Charlie Morris would be able to stop it. Morris was able to picture with all the clarity of despair the sleepless, worrying nights, the baffling helplessness, the dreary sensation of the next morning. It would mean a lot of trouble, and it would be very hurtful to that vanity of his which he would have termed his self-respect had he devoted a thought to it.

'Oh, my God!' said Morris again, having worked up to this climax. But Mary Morris said nothing. She only went on darning socks.

'You're sure about this?' demanded Morris. 'Quite sure? How do you know?'

'Of course I'm sure,' said Mary bitterly. 'The usual way. I haven't made a mistake.'

'When was it?'

'Six weeks ago. I expect it was – don't you remember that time?'

'Six weeks ago,' said Morris, counting on his fingers. 'December, January, February—'

'It'll be the end of August as near as makes no matter,' said Mary, cutting him short.

'End of August,' said Morris, with his mind racing once more over the intervening months, through that summer when he had expected to achieve so much in the advertising world, up to the time when bullying nurses would arrive and expenses would be so heavy, and on again to the time of nightly wailings and cryings. His thoughts moved in a harassing circle.

'Oh, confound it!' said Morris. 'Can't you – can't you do something about it?'

'What do you mean?' asked his wife sharply.

'You know. People do, sometimes. I've heard—'

'No, I can't,' said Mary with decision. 'I'm not going to make myself a wreck for life like Mrs Bartlett, if that's what you mean.'

If truth must be told, that was only part of Mary's motive, and the least part, too. Even though she herself disliked the new turn events had taken, even though she had dreaded breaking the news to her husband, she found much to reconcile herself to the prospect. Already it had brought her well into the forefront of her husband's attention, and that pleased her very decidedly. These recent evenings, when her husband had totally ignored her, had been beyond the reach of her chidings as of her affection, had begun to annoy her, had irked her sense of self-assertion. If by having a child she could once more claim something of her husband's attention, that in itself made it worth while. Not merely that, but she would have grounds for thinking more about herself than before; she would be able to spend her uninteresting days pondering over her symptoms and her development. It would be something happening in a world where far too little happened for her taste. And, anyway, far in the depths of her there was something which was curiously pleased at the prospect of having another child; just by that, without further consideration.

'No,' said Mary, 'I'm not going to do anything like that.'

And will met will in the glances which were exchanged across the fireside, and Charlie Morris, the great Charlie Morris, was forced to give way to the firm decision in his wife's eyes. He looked away uncomfortably and turned his gaze, as ever, back into the depths of the fire. His thoughts fled off once more round the circle of worrying pictures he called up among the glowing coals – of degrading work, and expense, and anxiety, and exertion, and of overbearing nurses, and sleepless nights, and humiliating helplessness before a crying baby. As if he had not enough to worry him at present!

His thoughts flew out of their vicious circle at an abrupt tangent. He had forgotten, with the shock of his wife's news all about Oldroyd, but now he remembered Oldroyd again. An hour ago, as he walked up from the station, he had been planning to kill Oldroyd. Oldroyd was a possible danger and a present annoyance at a time when he was pestered with annoyance. Morris set his teeth and began to feel a fierce satisfaction in the contemplation of the killing of Oldroyd. That would be some compensation for all his present trials. He felt he would like to tear Oldroyd to pieces with his hands, or stamp on him with his feet; he wanted to do something which would act as an outlet to all the irritation which was accumulating at high pressure within him. But that sort of violence was, of course, denied to him. It would be the equivalent of suicide on his part. He must not risk hanging just for the satisfaction of murdering Oldroyd in a comforting kind of way. He must devise some other plan for the abolishing of Oldroyd, even if it did not give him quite so much satisfaction. He must – and Morris straightway found himself plunged in a maze of thoughts leading, or designed to lead, to the same difficult end as he had had in contemplation when he was on his way home. Those thoughts did not lead him far. As has already been pointed out, one of the most difficult problems to a man living in a civilized town is how to plan a murder which will not incriminate him. Morris's brain that night was not very fertile in expedients. He could not devise a plan which he could consider satisfactory. There was some excuse for him, because every now and again his train of thought would be roughly intruded upon by the memory of the new worry which the evening had brought him. Backwards and forwards went his thoughts from Oldroyd to Mary, and from Mary to Oldroyd, as unsatisfactorily and as irritatingly as they well could. There were moments when he was almost sorry for himself, but those instants of self-pity were short-lived. Morris had changed a good deal lately, and nowadays his opinion of himself was too inflated for him to feel self-pity for long. At every setback to his sequence of thoughts he only set his jaw harder and contemplated the difficulties before him with an unabashed eye.

Some folk might say that the fierce resolution and stern determination which he displayed were comparable with those of Drake or Wellington. They might (if they were of the kind of person who always tries to find some good in everyone) say that Morris was displaying quite good qualities; that there was good stuff somewhere in Morris, and that it was a pity that his designs had taken a criminal turn. But it seems as if that argument is faulty. It seems much more probable that Morris was a born criminal, and solely a criminal, and that the ingenious plans he was able to form were only ingenious as long as he was inspired by hatred and irritation. It is hard to imagine Charlie Morris contributing to the good of the world. The ingenuity which killed Reddy and the resolution which killed Harrison have nothing in common with the daring which took the *Golden Hind* round the world, or the courage which held the squares together at Waterloo.

## CHAPTER XIV

During the days that followed Oldroyd's fear of Morris and his uncomfortable reaction towards the very unusual circumstanes in which he found himself displayed themselves in a sulky, lazy insolence towards Morris which bade fair to disorganize the whole running of the Universal Advertising Agency. The other young men working in the room could not help but notice Oldroyd's behaviour. Not unnaturally they tried to imitate it, and when Morris called them sharply to order they resented it, and sulked, and whispered to each other of favouritism. Mr Campbell, who noticed much more than an unobservant person would give him credit for, was early aware of this deplorable state of affairs. Matters were brought to a climax one morning when he suddenly appeared in the copy room and asked for some work which he had left to be done the day before.

'Oh, yes,' said Morris. 'Oldroyd, have you got those keyed figures out yet?'

'Not yet,' said Oldroyd. He said it a little uncomfortably, because he had not known that the work was something which Mr Campbell had specially ordered.

'Not done it *yet?*' demanded Mr Campbell. 'It ought to have been finished hours ago. What have you been up to since yesterday morning?'

'Well—' began Oldroyd doubtfully. He was not an accomplished liar. 'I had one or two other things to do as well—'

'Stuff and nonsense!' said Mr Campbell with extreme annoyance. 'I wanted them most particularly by this morning. I can't imagine what you've been thinking about. Mr Morris, see that you bring them in to me, tabulated in the way I asked you, in half an hour's time.'

Those tabulated figures were on Mr Campbell's desk, sure enough, half an hour later – the result of half an hour's work at high pressure by everyone in the copy room, driven on by the unsparing lash of Morris's tongue.

'Ah, thank you,' said Mr Campbell, taking up the ruled slips and glancing through them as Morris put them on his desk. 'Now, tell me, Morris, why weren't they ready when I wanted them?'

He peered at Morris kindly across his desk with his short-sighted eyes, but Morris knew that the kindliness in those mild blue eyes could change at short notice to keen anger, and he chose his words warily.

'I don't think Oldroyd thought there was any need for hurry yesterday, sir,' he said; 'he was a bit rushed with several jobs on hand.'

'What jobs?' demanded Mr Campbell.

He launched the question on the tail of Morris's last words, a shade too quickly even for Morris, who was playing for time. It was not surprising that Morris faltered before replying, nor that Mr Campbell noticed it.

'I don't believe a word of it,' said Mr Campbell. 'In my opinion that boy's bone lazy. It may be decent of you to stand

104

up for him because he's an old friend of yours, but it's not business. I wouldn't mind seeing him out of this office for good and all. He's upsetting the rest.'

Mr Campbell drummed with his fingers on his desk while he eyed Morris keenly to see how the suggestion would be received. Into Morris's mind's eye there flashed an instant picture of Oldroyd, fiercely on the defensive, with his upper lip curled back from his teeth, snarling out 'King's Evidence!' in reply to Morris's threats on just the same subject some time before. Oldroyd would do that, he would go and blurt out the whole affair to the police, if he were pushed to it by dismissal. At all costs the risk must not be run.

'Oh, no, sir,' said Morris, 'I shouldn't do that, sir. He's as good a copy clerk as you'll get anywhere. I'm quite satisfied with him.'

It irked Morris, the keen advertising man, inexpressibly to stand up in this fashion for the man who was disorganizing the whole office. His hatred of Oldroyd became more embittered than ever in that instant.

'M'm,' said Mr Campbell. 'It's your funeral, after all; it's you who has to run the copy room, not me. And I suppose you know Oldroyd better than I do. If you care to put up with him a bit longer I won't say no. But, mark my words, I don't think you're right about him. And the next time he does anything which puts me out, like what happened this morning, it's the sack for him. You'd better tell him so.'

'Right,' said Morris. 'I will.'

He had no intention whatever of doing so, however.

It is possible that all these accumulated worries had unsettled Morris, or that he would not have been, however advantageously situated, a good enough actor to conceal his emotions at this time. Oldroyd glanced sharply round at him as he came back into the copy room; he saw the cloud on Morris's brow, the thick eyebrows drawn together in the fierce scowl which (Oldroyd was well aware) boded no good to someone. And if Morris were plotting mischief against anyone, the chances were overwhelming that his intended victim was Oldroyd. That, of course, meant nothing particularly novel to Oldroyd. He was well enough aware of Morris's enmity. He had gone for weeks now with the knowledge that Morris would gladly see him dead. That knowledge, and the oppression of guilt and danger on account of the consequences of Harrison's murder, had done much towards unsettling Oldroyd in his work. He could not divide his life into watertight compartments as could Morris. He could not shake off his premonition of trouble; it disturbed him and interfered with his capacity for consecutive thought. Then his hatred and dislike for Morris was another disturbing factor. He could not apply himself with any zest at all to work which had been given him by Morris's thick hands. He even found that he could not work in the same room as Morris.

It would not have been so bad if the work-table had been so arranged that he faced Morris. Oldroyd could stand up to any danger he could see and guard against as well as any man; but it was a strain to sit at his table all day long with the knowledge that Morris was sitting only a few feet behind his back, eyeing him, most probably, and planning mischief. To Oldroyd's mental eye the pictured form of Morris's thick-shouldered body swelled sometimes to immense proportions. He seemed to Oldroyd to become like some huge poisonous spider, gorged with blood, crouching at his desk plotting the destruction of further victims. Oldroyd sometimes felt Morris's gaze piercing into the back of his head. He learned – although he did not know it – the meaning of the expression 'creeping of the flesh,' for when he had the impression that Morris was staring at him from behind he felt the hair rise on the back of his neck and the muscles beneath his skin tauten without his volition. It says much for Oldroyd's fear of unemployment that he was ready to endure this slow torture, and not resign from the office and seek a job in another where he would not be subjected to this kind of trial.

The point was that Oldroyd was influenced by another factor still. His sturdy north-country obstinacy was roused. To leave the office would have been a meek yielding to Morris, because Oldroyd knew that there was nothing Morris would like better than to see him go. Oldroyd's determination crystallized at the thought. Whatever it cost him, he would cling on to his place in the Universal Advertising Agency, and he would thwart Morris's plans at every opportunity. No wonder there was small tranquillity in the copy room.

This morning the tension was obvious to everyone. It must have been conveyed telepathically to Howlett and Lamb and Miss Campbell and the others, because they were acutely aware of it. Everyone felt uncomfortable and fidgeted in their chairs.

It was with a sigh of relief that Miss Campbell rose to go out to lunch with her father.

'You can spare my daughter's services for an hour, Mr Morris, I take it?' said Mr Campbell with his usual jocularity.

Morris did not display his usual appreciation of Mr Campbell's kind condescension. He merely nodded, with hardly a glance at his employer. His chin was on his hand, and he was staring straight in front of him at the window, evidently deep in thought. Mr Campbell believed that his thoughts were directed towards the betterment of the Universal Advertising Agency, and was accordingly gratified. But he was wrong; Morris was forming other plans entirely. The creative mood was on him. The few glances he directed at Oldroyd's back would have told a keen observer the object of the plans he was making.

Morris seemed to come to a decision. He sat back more comfortably in his chair.

'You can go and get your lunch now, Oldroyd,' he said ponderously, and, without a word, Oldroyd heaved himself out of his chair and began to put on his overcoat. Those two did not exchange more words than were necessary nowadays. As the door closed behind him Morris rose from his chair as well.

'I'm going to get my lunch, too,' he announced. 'Howlett, you're in charge. If that bally mustard man comes in tell him I'll be back at two.'

Then he went out hastily, and, clattering down the stairs in a violent hurry, he overtook Oldroyd just as that young man was turning the corner to walk up the Strand.

'I wanted to talk to you, old man,' said Morris.

Oldroyd did not seem in the least delighted to hear it. He looked round at Morris and then continued on his way without a word. But he was thoroughly on his guard. He had seen the look on Morris's face when the latter emerged from Mr Campbell's room; more than that Morris was addressing him, ingratiatingly, as 'old man,' and that, Oldroyd felt instinctively, was a sure indication of approaching trouble. He was keyed up ready to face danger, whatever that danger might be, although even Oldroyd had no idea how pressingly close the danger lay.

'Old Mac's cutting up pretty rusty, you know,' said Morris, striding along beside Oldroyd. 'He spoke about giving you the sack this morning, and he would have done it, too, if I hadn't spoken up for you.'

Oldroyd only condescended to answer with a grunt and a

quickening of his pace. The pavement was packed with lunch-time crowds, and the two had to thread their way along at the edge of the curb, while the big red buses roared by at Oldroyd's elbow – Morris had taken up a position on the inside.

'Now look here, old man,' said Morris pleadingly, 'you mustn't let us both down like this. It's dam' bad for the office when you slack about. You can take it for sure that if old Mac's noticed it everyone else has, too. It's bad for both of us.'

'M'm,' said Oldroyd; it was barely audible through the roar of the traffic.

'Try and pull yourself together, old man,' said Morris. 'Look at me. *I* don't let things interfere with my work, do I? Please, old man—'

He put his big right hand upon Oldroyd's shoulder and strode along beside him, pushing past the sauntering crowd. The touch of his hand roused Oldroyd's loathing. He shuddered a little under it, but he made no attempt to throw it off. He was still keyed up, looking for a trap in what Morris was saying, innocent though it appeared.

'Please, old man,' said Morris. There was humility in his tone, which set Oldroyd all the more on his guard.

'Please,' said Morris, and his hand on Oldroyd's shoulder moved a little, as though settling itself more firmly. It was that which saved Oldroyd's life in all probability. Morris had been stealing glances back over his right shoulder. For a space there had been little traffic; now a motor-bus came racing up close to the kerb, not a yard from Oldroyd. As it reached him Morris straightened his arm. It was a straight, well-timed push that he gave him; it would have been just enough, had not Oldroyd been on his guard, to send him off the pavement straight under the wheels of the bus. It would have been simple enough; people step in dozens every month off the pavements of London straight under motor-bus wheels, and the crowded state of the pavement would have appeared ample enough explanation of such a movement by Oldroyd.

Morris gave the thrust and whipped his hand back to his side; it was a carefully thought out movement, and no one of the disinterested crowd would have thought twice about it, not even if a fatal accident had resulted. But Oldroyd was not killed. That momentary settling of Morris's grip on his shoulder had given him a subconscious warning. He staggered

108

forwards rather than sideways when the thrust came. He reeled for a second on the brink of the kerb. The driver of the bus shouted and tried to swerve, but the danger was over before the driver could have done anything to forestall it. Oldroyd tottered for a moment and then came back well on to the pavement. His eyes met Morris's, and he turned slightly sick at the glare of bestial ferocity which he perceived there.

Morris opened and shut his mouth, but he could utter no sound. In this early humiliation of his first failure he was not able to act impromptu. He was ready and prepared to be horrified and afflicted when his dear friend was run over, but he could not change his part with ease at this short notice. It was four or five seconds before he had control over himself again.

'Steady, old man,' he said; 'there'll be an accident if you're not careful.'

'What in hell do you mean?' spluttered Oldroyd.

'Why,' said Morris, 'you nearly walked underneath that bus. You ought to look where you're going. Really you ought.'

'But you pushed me!' expostulated Oldroyd. 'You pushed me! You devil!'

They were still in the midst of the hurrying crowds of the Strand. Not one of the many scores of passers-by had the least idea that they had very nearly been witnesses of a brutal and well-planned murder. They did not know that the burly flamboyant young man with the tilted bowler had two dreadful crimes on his soul, any more than they knew that he had planned to make the slight little chap with the scrubby moustache beside him his next victim, or any more than they knew that the pair of them were in heated argument about the last attempt.

'Hold hard,' said Morris. 'You mustn't say such things about me. You mustn't.'

'Mustn't I! And why not? It's the truth, isn't it? You know it is?'

Morris gave up the attempt to appear innocent.

'Well, supposing it is. What of it?' he demanded, and Oldroyd found it difficult to say anything in reply. He could only look at Morris. Then abruptly Morris turned on his heel and walked away, leaving Oldroyd staring after him. It was a wordless declaration of war, issued, as is not unusual, after the opening of hostilities. To Oldroyd, gazing after Morris's striding form, came the realization that he was in deadly peril and

109

that he had only himself to rely upon for his safety. From now onward he was engaged in a duel with Morris, a duel to the death with a fiend of strength and cunning. He felt fearful and shaken.

## CHAPTER XV

When Morris returned from his lunch his first act was to send his other assistants out to have theirs; he was always careful as far as possible of the comfort and well-being of his juniors. Possibly he may also have been influenced by his desire for solitude for the purpose of undisturbed thought. He sat down in Clarence's chair; he turned over idly a few of the latter's drawings and then lost himself in a maze of badly co-ordinated thought as he gazed out of the window. The bitterness of failure soon became much less acute. His vanity was sufficient to disguise it. It had been a good plan, well conceived and ably prepared. Why, he had made use, as ever, of the smallest scraps of circumstantial evidence. Had Oldroyd died that lunch-time, and had by any chance suspicion fallen upon him, there was not a man or woman in that office who would not have been prepared to swear that Oldroyd was a favourite and a friend of his, in whose favour he was always ready to stretch a point of office discipline. He had foreseen that anyone who observed the push he gave Oldroyd would never have been able to swear for certain that it was a push, and not an unsuccessful attempt to pull him back.

The brilliance and soundness of the plan soon reconciled Morris to its failure. If anything, his opinion of himself was enhanced rather than diminished. His self-confidence came to his rescue. It would not be long before he could devise and execute another and more successful plan for the annihilation of Oldroyd. He felt the germs of several ideas sprouting in his mind already. He went over them carefully, weeding out the unpromising ones. The remainder he left to germinate still further in the watertight compartment mind of his before he should return to them. Having reached that satisfactory conclusion, he was quite ready to turn back again to normal office life at the very time when Miss Campbell came into the copy room again.

'Hullo!' said Morris.

'Hullo!' said Miss Campbell. She bestowed upon him her own particular charming smile, for Miss Campbell was not above trying to captivate this young man who had the supervision of her daily work, and in whose power largely lay the means to make her days comfortable or the reverse.

'The usual good lunch, I suppose?' asked Morris, with his very best manners.

'Of course,' said Miss Campbell.

'And the usual good appetite?' asked Morris with what he considered epigrammatic brilliancy.

'The result of the usual good conscience,' replied Miss Campbell.

'Lucky girl,' said Morris.

'Why, isn't your conscience as good as it might be?' asked Miss Campbell.

'No, I'm afraid not,' replied Morris, but he did not mean anything like what a person who knew all about his doings would have thought he meant; on the contrary, Morris felt his conscience to be singularly clear, and only said the opposite in order to begin a good gambit in the delicious game of badinage with his employer's daughter.

'Dear, dear,' said Miss Campbell. She spoke ironically, but she was still young enough to be impressed by a man of thirty admitting to a guilty conscience.

'Whatever have you been up to?' asked Miss Campbell.

'Oh, things I couldn't tell you about,' answered Morris, beaming benignantly.

'Goodness! You must have been badly brought up,' said Miss Campbell, her grey eyes wide, but with a smile in them. By this remark she gave Morris exactly the opening which his gambit had played for.

'Yes,' said Morris, 'I'm afraid I came under bad influence when I was young. I hadn't met *you* then, you see.'

'And what difference would that have made, pray?' asked Miss Campbell. It was the inevitable move in reply to Morris's.

'Ah!' said Morris. 'I think you would have had a good influence over me if we had met when I was young.'

His tone implied that he did not mean what he said; his eyes implied that he did.

For a moment Miss Campbell's sense of humour nearly spoilt the situation; balancing her nineteen years against Morris's thirty, she saw herself in short frocks at the age of seven, when Morris was eighteen. But the temptation to go on flirting with her boss was too strong for her.

'Dear me!' said Miss Campbell. 'What a pity Fate has held us apart, isn't it?'

'Yes,' said Morris, and his lustrous eyes burnt into Miss Campbell's grey ones. Morris had a personality which could make itself felt; Doris certainly was well aware of the impact of his glance. She dropped her eyes, and there was an odd, curiously effective silence for a second or two. It was broken when Morris rose carelessly from Clarence's chair.

'Oh, well,' he said, moving slowly across the room, 'time remedies everything in the end, doesn't it? Perhaps—'

But it can never be known what Morris was going to say next, for his sentence was cut short by the opening of the door and the entry of Oldroyd. Morris did not complete his sentence, and Oldroyd felt as he entered that he was cutting short someone's speech, and felt intrusive and uncomfortable in consequence. His glance observed Miss Campbell at her table, and Morris lounging over to her, and he realized in what manner he had been intrusive. Even Miss Campbell, sitting at her table, felt an oddly annoying sensation of being caught. As for Morris, the glance he shot at Oldroyd told exactly how annoyed he was. Oldroyd mumbled something which a person of extremely quick ear might have guessed to be 'Good afternoon,' and hastened to his own place, while Miss Campbell proceeded to shuffle the papers on her table with unnecessary violence. It was, she felt, a ridiculous thing to feel self-conscious about – but there was no denying that Morris now had firmly caught her attention. He was to her now far more of a distinct individual than the elegant young men she met at dances in the evenings, despite the coarseness of his looks and the twang of his accent.

Morris himself sat at his desk and allowed his thoughts to wander away from advertising and murder to love and success. Doris Campbell was undeniably a pretty little thing. She had a sprightliness and spirit which were in great contrast with those his wife displayed. She had unspoiled good looks, while his wife was lined and careworn. His wife had brought him nothing on their marriage, and a comparison between the dates of their

112

wedding and of Molly Morris's birth would have told much of the story of the motive of the marriage. Doris, on the other hand, was his employer's daughter, and there was no son. Morris was well aware of the advantages a keen young advertising man would enjoy if he were the son-in-law of Mr Campbell, majority shareholder and managing director of the Universal Advertising Agency. But that necessarily implied marriage – anything less than marriage would be decidedly dangerous and disadvantageous, and Morris was a married man already. With any other married man the line of thought might well have ended there and then, although it was quite a likely one to be pursued so far. But with Morris it meant going a little farther. It being a case of an urgent desire on his part, he was not of the stuff to be deterred by apparent difficulties from trying to gratify it. Ideas began to sprout again in his mind, although even he found those ideas so terrible that he flinched from working them out fully. Yet in time to come, when he had acquired familiarity with those ideas, he might not find them quite so distasteful. Morris suspected that at that very moment, and he was almost glad when the return of Howlett and the others interrupted his line of thought. He started them briskly on their work and plunged into his own part of it with zest. During the afternoon he hardly interrupted himself at all to scowl across the room at Oldroyd's unresponsive back.

As for that young man, his brain was plunged into such a torment of thought that he did less than ever towards earning the salary paid him by the Universal Advertising Agency. His hands were still quivering a little after the shock he had undergone at lunch-time; he had been within an inch of death then, and it was an unpleasing novel experience. All the same, he did not fear nor hate the thought of death one half as much as he feared and hated Morris. He hated him for his cunning and his strength, just as he hated him for his coarse features and his thick hands and his burly shoulders and his greasy curls. Oldroyd felt half sick with his violent personal loathing for Morris. And added to that was his new suspicion that something was developing between Morris and Miss Campbell. Allowance must be made for Oldroyd's unbalanced state of mind. By this time his suspicion of Morris was so acute that he tended to regard the simplest action on Morris's part as inspired by sinister motives. He felt his muscles brace themselves even when Morris addressed some casual remark to Clarence or

Shepherd. What deep plan Morris had under consideration with regard to Miss Campbell, Oldroyd could not even guess. He felt there was a plan, all the same. And, being frightened, Oldroyd could not help but think that it was a plan tending to his own hurt, and he became more frightened still. But Oldroyd had the highest kind of courage. The more frightened he felt, the tighter he stuck to his post. He refused to allow Morris to get the better of him.


## CHAPTER XVI


For a full month life went on at the Universal Advertising Agency and in the home of Mr Charles Morris with only gradual change. Morris relapsed into his self-contained abstraction, which was becoming habitual to him at home. His wife noticed it, of course, but without paying particular attention to it. So far she had not been compelled to make any unusual demand upon his good nature or his patience. She was accustomed to his moody periods of thought.

Nor was it surprising that Morris should be moody and thoughtful. He had enough, far more than enough, to keep any normal mind fully occupied. Besides the question of gratifying his main hatred of the moment, he had the beginnings of another scheme in his mind. Then there was his flirtation (it had grown to that by now) with Miss Campbell. Last of all, he was working out the details of a scheme which was not to be officially regarded as a crime against society – his Ultra-violet Soap Bonus Scheme.

That was a really brilliant idea. The germs of it had been in his mind for some time, and now, despite his other preoccupations (or very likely because of them), they had begun to multiply and divide, until it was not very long before the complete idea was formulated. It was a really wonderful scheme, presenting all the desirable qualities an advertising idea could possibly have in the present state of society. It was original – and originality stands at the same premium in the advertising world as it commands everywhere else. It was simple. It would stimulate the sales of Ultra-violet Soap at the same time as it would start talk about it. It did not possess the radical defect of the great Mustard Club movement, because it would not stimulate the sale of other soaps besides Ultra-violet. Most important of all, from Morris's point of view, was the fact that it would induce the proprietors of that commodity to spend more money through the Universal Advertising Agency, thereby increasing that firm's commission and raising the standing of the originator of the idea even higher than it stood at present.

Morris never had a moment's doubt about the acceptance or the success of the plan. Both were clearly obvious and inevitable. Soon Morris was ready to put the scheme before higher authority, but with acute business caution he kept it to himself for a few days longer; he might think of some improvement; also, he might find a way of making his suggestion direct to the Ultra-violet Company and arranging for the matter to be entrusted solely to him – thereby setting himself up at once as a fully-established advertising agent with at least one opulent client. Yet all those golden day-dreams were soon to be shattered completely.

Mr Campbell was clearly in a bad temper. Morris himself had made one bad mistake lately, and the rest of the staff had done worse still. Howlett and Oldroyd had been subjected to censure not merely from Morris, but from Mr Campbell in person. Morris could tell by now in what mood he would find Mr Campbell when summoned into the presence; a short sharp call on the buzzer implied bad temper, while a longer one meant good temper. It was a short sharp call which brought him into the managing director's room that afternoon.

'What the dickens does this mean?' demanded Mr Campbell irritably. He brandished a sheaf of papers under Morris's nose as the latter came to a stand by his chair. Morris looked, and his heart sank.

'That's the simplest job there is in the whole office, and some fool's made a mess of it. Who the devil is there who can't do simple proportion sums? Who is it who makes six inches at thirty shillings an inch six pounds ten?'

Morris knew at once, but he found it impossible to answer in words.

'Whose writing is this?' demanded Mr Campbell. 'Oldroyd's, isn't it? I thought as much. Well, that's the last time he makes an ass of himself in this office. God only knows how many mistakes there are in this lot. I've found three myself already. Out he goes, Morris, soon as we decently can. We'll give him a fortnight to find another job in, and a week's pay after that if he hasn't got one, and that's the last of him.

Mr Campbell was in the blaze of furious passion one would not expect to see in a mild tempered Scot. He hammered on his desk to accentuate his words, while Morris was incapable of reply. His own business sense was too acute for him to find any argument whatever in favour of Oldroyd.

'Go and fetch him in,' commanded Mr Campbell. 'Fetch him at once, and we'll settle this business out of hand.'

Morris started to go, checked himself, moved again, halted again. He could not bring himself to the fatal action of being a party to the dismissal of Oldroyd.

'Sorry to hurt your feelings,' said Mr Campbell, milder already at the prospect of action, 'but it's got to be done, hasn't it, now?'

Morris saw one possible way of averting catastrophe, and he seized the opportunity. It was an enormous sacrifice, but it had to be gone through.

'It's not that, sir,' said Morris, 'but Oldroyd's a better man than you'd think.'

'You've said that before, and I don't believe it,' said Mr Campbell with a snort.

'Well, sir,' said Morris, 'I know what's been making him so absentminded lately.'

'Well, what?'

'He only started telling me this morning. It's like this.' And in a few glib words Morris reeled off the whole essentials of the Ultra-violet Soap Bonus Scheme. It was clear proof of its soundness as an advertising idea that it could be expressed in such a brief speech.

'Hm,' said Mr Campbell, clearly moved by the brilliance of the idea, 'there's a lot in that, as you say. But what about—'

He asked a pertinent question which showed the rapidity with which he had grasped the point.

'Oh, there's no difficulty there, sir,' said Morris. 'You simply—' His explanation called for very few words.

'Yes, I see,' said Mr Campbell. Then he suddenly saw more still, saw the whole beauty of the scheme spread before him. 'And, by George, it'll be easy enough to—' What he said showed how deeply he was enchanted by the prospect.

116

'So you think there's something in it, sir?' asked Morris.

'Something in it! There's a gold mine in it. I can't think why no one's ever thought of it before. Do you mean to tell me it was that lad Oldroyd who got this idea?'

'I think so, sir. He hasn't spoken to me about it before to-day.'

'Why, it's wonderful! I would never have thought he had it in him. It'll be the biggest thing this office has ever done.'

'So you think the Ultra-violet Soap people will take it up?'

'Positive. Certain. You and I know that clients are all damned fools, Morris, but no client would be such a damned fool as to let this go by. Go and get young Oldroyd, and I'll tell him that I'll take it up with the Ultra-violet people.'

That was a new facer for Morris. He knew Oldroyd would be quite incapable of taking up the mysterious cues which would be rained on him the moment he came into the room.

'Well, sir, I shouldn't do that if I were you. You see – you see – Oldroyd only told me this in confidence this morning. I wouldn't have told you now if you hadn't been going to give him the sack. He wouldn't like it if he knew I'd told you without his permission.'

'Oh, yes,' said Mr Campbell. 'Quite, quite. I see. Well, what are you going to do about it?'

'Um. I think the best I can do is to talk to him this evening and get him to agree to my telling you. I thought this morning that you'd like the idea, but I couldn't be sure.'

'Not be sure, man? That's not like you, Morris. It's a brilliant idea. I thought you'd have jumped to it at once. It's going to be the making of us. Goodness only knows how that boy Oldroyd came to work it all out so neatly.'

Every word Mr Campbell said only twisted the barb more deeply in Morris's wound. It had been maddening to lose the credit and the possible cash for his cherished idea; it was more maddening still to see all this credit bestowed upon a dolt like Oldroyd. And worst of all was it to be censured, however indirectly, for not having the brains to see the beauty of the plan immediately. What with the strain and annoyance, Morris was nearly beside himself. It may have been fortunate that Mr Campbell was too enchanted with the new idea to notice anything specially odd about his manner.

'Very well, then,' said Mr Campbell. 'Speak to him about it tonight, so that you can tell me officially tomorrow.'

And with that Morris emerged from the managing director's room, hot and uncomfortable under his collar, and with a perfect volcano of suppressed rage within him.

At half-past five the people in the copy room were beginning their usual unobtrusive packing up, ready for instant departure as soon as Morris should give the word.

'Right,' said Morris; his throat was dry with excitement and his voice sounded strained. 'Miss Campbell you can push off now. And I don't think I want Clarence or Howlett any more. Have you got those files finished, Lamb? Good man! Off you go, then. Right ho, Shepherd. Don't be more than ten minutes late tomorrow, will you? Sorry, Oldroyd, but we'll have to stay a bit this evening and run through those letters Anthony wanted sent off for him. Maudie's only just brought them in.'

Oldroyd forced himself to turn and look at Morris. He had, of course, not the least knowledge of what had passed this afternoon between Morris and Mr Campbell. All he knew was that Morris was a little excited, and that he had found a not very convincing excuse to keep him back alone in the office with him. It is very uncomfortable to foresee oneself left alone in an isolated office with a man who has attempted your life once, and whom you know to be ready to attempt it again.

'I can't stop tonight,' said Oldroyd feebly, which was just what Morris expected him to say.

'Sorry, but you'll have to. It's only for a minute,' said Morris incisively.

The others in the room looked at Oldroyd with small sympathy. They were delighted to hear the favourite being treated with so much brusqueness.

'Come up here,' said Morris, 'and let's get started, since you're in such a hurry.'

Oldroyd could not protest further, literally not to save his life. There are certain things one cannot do in the public life of an office. With dragging steps Oldroyd mounted the dais to Morris's table, and then he sat down in the chair that Morris indicated to him.

'Well, good night,' said Lamb, and he and Shepherd clattered out. They were the last of the staff left in the office save for Morris and Oldroyd.

With their departure Oldroyd shifted his chair uneasily out of reach of Morris. He sat crouched forward, awaiting some new attack planned by Morris with his usual devilish cunning.

Morris noticed the tension of his attitude, and was irritated and amused in equal proportions. It is gratifying to be considered a dangerous man, but annoying when it interferes with one's plans, especially when one's plans are being developed very much against one's grain.

'Confound it,' said Morris. 'Don't be so hellish careful. I'm not going to kill you this evening.'

That assurance, as was to be expected, counted absolutely for nothing with Oldroyd. He did not relax in the least.

'Now pay attention to what I'm going to say,' said Morris.

Oldroyd said nothing, nor did his expression change.

'Mac wanted to give you the sack this afternoon. It's not the first time, you know. He spoke about it to me a week or two ago. Do you remember?'

Oldroyd was not at all likely to forget that particular day.

'Well,' went on Morris, 'he wanted to call you in and give you the sack then and there, and there was only one way in which I could stop him: I had to tell him all about a scheme I had made up and say it was your idea.'

So far Oldroyd did not grant the least credence to what Morris had said. He took it for granted that this was all part of a scheme for his undoing.

'The idea was this—' said Morris, and he went on to describe, for the second time that day, the epoch-making Ultra-violet Soap Bonus Scheme.

Oldroyd, who had worked in various advertising offices since he was sixteen, could hardly help but be impressed. He could not but admire the neat and inexpensive manner in which the attention of the Press, and the public, and the retailers was to be immediately caught. His face displayed a flicker of interest. Whatever designs Morris had on his life, he had certainly presented him gratis with a flawless idea worth a great deal of money and prestige to any advertising man.

'Yes,' snarled Morris, 'that's the idea I had to give away to Mac and say it was yours, you—'

Morris called Oldroyd several names in quick succession; each name was unpleasant and filthy. Oldroyd did not mind in the least.

'Well, damn you,' asked Morris, 'haven't you got anything to say?'

'Not yet,' said Oldroyd, wooden as ever.

'Anyway,' said Morris, 'that's what I told Mac this afternoon. Of course he fell for the idea straight away – of course he did, blast you. He wanted to have you in and tell you he'd taken it up, and I had to stop him by saying that you'd only told me in confidence. So tomorrow I've got to tell him you've given me permission to tell him. Do you understand?'

'I heard what you've said to me,' said Oldroyd cautiously.

'Oh, blast you, *blast* you!' said Morris. 'Aren't you going to back me up?'

'I don't know about that.'

Oldroyd probably had never heard any proverbial saying about the giving of Greek gifts, but he was acting with a caution which seemed to show that he had.

'But you must; you must,' said Morris.

Morris of the iron nerve was finding all this strain too much even for him. The possibility that he might have thrown away his splendid idea to no purpose at all drove him almost hysterical, and the prospect of the complications which would ensue in the morning if Oldroyd disowned the authorship of the scheme was still more fuel added to the flames.

'I don't see any must about it,' said Oldroyd sturdily.

Morris beat with his fists on the table. He used vile language. Oldroyd found a certain amount of pleasure in the spectacle. It was some sort of repayment for all the trouble Morris had caused him recently.

Then with a huge effort Morris engulfed his impotent rage in a fatalistic resignation.

'Well, if you won't you won't,' he said. 'I've done all I could. If you don't back me up I shall be in a bit of a mess, but not half so bad a mess as you. You'll get the sack, although I've tried to save you. And if you care to go bleating to the police I can't stop you. So that's that. Anyway, when Mac calls you into his room tomorrow you'll know what it's for, so you needn't make a fool of yourself unless you want to.'

'I'll see that it's not me who's made a fool of,' said Oldroyd.

Morris's rage bade fair to overmaster him again. He was on the verge of giving it vent by hurling himself in a wild physical attack on the slight little man who was causing all this trouble, but his common sense told him that it would be hard to find circumstances more dangerous in which to commit murder. Oldroyd saw the possibility and held himself in readiness. Then Morris made a little gesture of surrender.

'Oh, clear out!' he said at last. 'Get out of here before I kill you!'

Oldroyd slid his chair cautiously to the edge of the dais before he stood up. He did not turn his back on Morris for a moment while he reached for his hat and coat and sidled through the door. Until he had gone, and for some minutes afterwards, Morris sat on at his table, drumming with his fingers and staring out into the darkness beyond the windows.


## CHAPTER XVII


Next morning at the office it may or may not have been obvious that Morris had passed a very bad night. Nobody observed him at all closely, for the people who were most likely to do so were far too excited. Mr Campbell had hardly seated himself at his desk, he had hardly made a pretence of glancing through the letters which Maudie brought in to him, before he pressed the button which summoned Morris into his room.

'Have you asked him yet?' he demanded as soon as Morris opened the door.

'Yes,' said Morris.

'And what did he say?'

'He said all right.'

'Fine! Call him in then, and let's get going.'

Morris opened the door and called Oldroyd into the presence.

'Mr Morris has told me,' said Mr Campbell, 'about this bonus scheme of yours for Ultra-violet Soap. It's a good idea. Quite a good idea.'

Morris stared anxiously at Oldroyd, wondering what he would say. He said nothing at present.

'In fact,' said Mr Campbell, 'I have decided to take it up with the company. I'm sure they'll agree.'

Oldroyd only nodded. It was not until that moment that he decided to fall in with Morris's plans. He had puzzled all night over the situation and had failed to discover any trap in it, or any chance of Morris doing any damage to him by it. All his serious thought had only gone to convince him that for once in a way Morris had been speaking the plain truth – and for once in a way, of course, that is just what Morris had been doing.

Mr Campbell was looking at Oldroyd in a puzzled kind of way. He expected him to show some kind of elation at this official endorsement of his suggestion, and was surprised to find no trace of such elation. But Mr Campbell was quite ready to dub the Oldroyd riddle as insoluble. If an apparently stolid, unimaginative, careless, lazy fellow like Oldroyd could produce the brilliant idea of the Ultra-violet Bonus Scheme, then there were bound to be other surprising points about his character and conduct. He gave up his internal debate.

'I'll get through to them now, I think,' he announced, and picked up his desk telephone.

'Get me Mr White of the Ultra-violet people,' he said over the instrument to Maudie in the outer office.

He put back the instrument on his desk and began to wander round the room, his hands deep in his trousers pockets, where they rattled incessantly his keys and coppers. He was very clearly in a state of excitement. When the bell rang he grabbed the telephone expectantly.

'Hullo!' he said. 'That you, White? Oh, I'm all right, thank you. Listen. I've got an idea. It's a winner, I think. Yes, I know, but this time you'll say the same when you hear about it. When can I see you? Oh, no, no, no, the quicker we get on to this the better. Have lunch with me today. Oh, that's a pity. Well, what are you doing just at this minute? That's all right. I expect you'll put him off when you hear what I've got to say. I'll get a taxi now. I'll be with you in ten minutes if they haven't got the Strand up again. Right. Goodbye. Where's my hat?'

With that Mr Campbell was gone; but what he had said over the telephone had told Morris and Oldroyd more eloquently than a dozen speeches just how highly Mr Campbell approved of the idea he believed to be Oldroyd's. The glances those two exchanged after his departure were just as eloquent from another point of view, although anyone ignorant of the details of the situation would have found it a difficult task to explain them.

Two hours later the buzzer at Morris's table sounded again – a long note, significant of Mr Campbell's good temper.

'Just as I said,' said Mr Campbell to Morris. 'White liked the idea straight away. We can start getting out a few roughs at once. White said the usual thing – have to consult his fellow directors and all that; but I know what White says goes with that firm every time. We can call it settled. Now, look here. What space are we going to take for this stunt? What about—'

There is no need to recount what Mr Campbell went on to discuss. It was a highly technical advertising matter, calling for frequent consultation of the statistics compiled from keyed advertisements, balancing of space charges against sales and all the other intricacies of the profession. Morris and Mr Campbell argued the matter back and forth with loving care, sketching out the huge noisy campaign in as much detail as experience could foresee. There was need for haste; Mr White wanted a complete scheme submitted to him that evening to tell his other directors about next day. So demand after demand went into the other room for figures and files and statistics. At one o'clock Morris hurried into the copy room for a moment, hurriedly looking over the work which had been done, distributed a few more urgent jobs, issued permission for lunch to be taken one at a time, twenty minutes each, and hastened back to continue the discussion with Mr Campbell. They lunched off a sketchy meal Shepherd brought in to them, and continued the debate with their mouths full. Once, and only once, did Oldroyd's name come up in the conversation.

'Look here,' said Campbell, conscience stricken, 'don't you think Oldroyd ought to be consulted a bit on this matter? It's his idea, you know.'

There was a guilty pause before Morris answered. Then:

'No,' said Morris. 'I don't expect he'd thank us if we asked him. And I don't think he'd be much good, anyway.'

'Neither do I,' said Mr Campbell in a relieved tone. 'I'll have to raise his wages, I suppose. But all he's good for is ideas apparently. He's got no head for detail.'

Both of them seemed to be very glad to agree on this point. In the full flood of campaign planning Mr Campbell felt that Oldroyd would be *de trop,* somehow, while Morris simply hated the thought of Oldroyd intruding further into this, his first big scheme. But during the discussion Morris's respect for Mr Campbell, and still more Mr Campbell's respect for Morris increased by leaps and bounds. They were filled with exaltation and mutual esteem.

Outside in the copy room the excitement grew with each further summons from the director's room. No one (except Old-royd) knew what was being planned; all they could guess was that it was something peculiarly promising and exciting. Even Miss Campbell knew no more than that, as she freely admitted. Morris was regarded with passionate interest by four pairs of eyes every time he appeared in the copy room, and debate ran high each time he came back again with a demand for some new data. In the end Oldroyd, who had been quietly working at his corner table, could not find any more patience for the discussion.

'I know what they're doing,' he said quietly.

Lamb and Howlett looked at him with disbelief.

'What is it?' they demanded.

'It's a bonus scheme for Ultra-violet. They're going to—' Once more the scheme was outlined in the premises of the Universal Advertising Agency. When he had heard it all Lamb whistled with admiration.

'That's a stunt, by George, now, isn't it?' he declared.

'Whose idea was it?' demanded Howlett. 'Morris's, I suppose. Sounds too good for the old man.'

'It wasn't either of them,' said Oldroyd.

'Well, who was it?' asked Lamb.

'Yes, who was it, Mr Oldroyd?' asked Miss Campbell.

'It was me,' said Oldroyd modestly, and a shocked silence greeted his words.

'Go on!' said Lamb.

'Tell us a few more like that,' said Howlett.

'It was, really,' said Oldroyd, a little nettled by this unbelief.

'Well, upon my sainted Sam,' said Howlett.

'Really and truly?' asked Miss Campbell.

'Yes,' said Oldroyd.

'Well, I think it was very clever of you,' said Miss Campbell, and it was obvious that everyone in the room agreed with her.

'Mac ought to raise your screw for that,' said Lamb.

'Perhaps he's done it already?' said Howlett.

'No, not yet,' said Oldroyd.

'Well, he will,' said Miss Campbell with decision.

'It's the biggest thing for years,' said Lamb, and the envy of his tone was balm to Oldroyd's soul.

'People will still be talking about you when you're dead and gone,' said Howlett.

The candidate for immortality almost blushed. He found

even this undeserved praise most intoxicating; the more so as he had felt rather a pariah lately in the office.

'We'll want a bigger staff now,' said Shepherd. Roseate visions were conjured up in his mind by those words. He might be promoted to copy writer and clerk, and another office boy might arrive for Shepherd to bully. That would be exceedingly pleasant.

'Promotion all round,' said Howlett. 'Bit of a bonus, too, perhaps.'

It was just what Mr Campbell was saying in other words to Morris at this very moment. 'Do you think you can handle this with the staff we've got?' he asked.

'M'm,' said Morris. 'No, I don't think I can.'

'Braithwaite was talking to me a couple of days ago,' said Mr Campbell. 'He's looking for a job. If he'd come to me three months back he could have had Harrison's, but of course I won't do anything like that now. Do you think you could use him?'

Braithwaite was a man of considerable reputation as a copy writer. There had been a time when Morris had looked up to him in awe. Now he thought the matter over calmly, without a quickening of the pulse.

'Yes, Braithwaite'll do,' he said.

Mr Campbell was tolerably impressed by his calm self-reliance. They went on to discuss the reorganization of the office, in which they came to decisions which sadly disappointed most of the staff with regard to promotion, although they were all to be gratified in a few week's time, when the Ultra-violet Scheme had attained its historic success, by a substantial bonus based on salary scales. Only Oldroyd was pleased with the knowledge of an immediate rise in wages.

Morris announced the forthcoming changes in the copy room with characteristic abruptness.

'Mr Campbell's taking the office across the corridor as well,' he said. 'There are three rooms there. That's where I'm going. Mr Braithwaite – you've heard of him, haven't you? – will be coming in here to look after you lot, except the ones who come with me. Clarence, I'll want you next door – Mr Braithwaite's bringing another artist here with him. There's another typist coming, too. She'll be over with me.'

He paused, while the others hung on his words. He could not control his voice properly as he said the next words. He knew he was going to announce a decision of the utmost importance to himself; why his voice changed was because he was not at all sure that it was altogether a wise one.

'And you'll be coming there, too, Miss Campbell,' he said.

Morris could have had Lamb, or Howlett, or Oldroyd, or even Shepherd for the matter of that. The first two were good average workers. Oldroyd might have been the wisest choice, when all was said and done. He would have been able to keep his eye on Oldroyd, and perhaps cover up some of his deficiencies. But he was yielding to his inclination and his ambitions. He wanted to have Miss Campbell with him. That was partly because he had grown to like having her at his side. But also it was because he wanted to establish himself well in her favour in case Fate should make him a widower. He already had a lurking suspicion that something like that might happen.


## CHAPTER XVIII


There is no need now to describe in detail the astounding success of the Ultra-violet Soap Distributive Bonus Scheme. That is a matter of advertising history now. It is quoted in manuals of the profession, and advertising men all the world over imitate its details slavishly. It was a lottery to which the police could not find any objection; the money distributed, which apparently came from the firm, actually came from the pockets of the public. It held the public spellbound; it sent up the sales of Ultra-violet Soap amazingly – as was only to be expected of a public who were quite prepared to believe in a connection (implied, though hardly expressed) between a perfume of violets and the benignant properties of ultra-violet light. The newspapers were forced to give it publicity it had not paid for. Soon the most definite proof of its renown was reached, when the Bonus Scheme became a subject for music-hall gags. Yet such was Mr Campbell's nature that he could never help commenting to himself, with a wry smile, on the incongruity which rewarded Oldroyd for his idea with a pound a week rise in salary at the same time as Mr Campbell himself was pocketing more than a hundred times as much.

But there was one person to whom this success was a source of irritation, and that, of course, was Morris. He threw himself heart and soul into the work of the scheme, as was his wont, but the more it succeeded (and it soon reached a pitch when it ran itself and it would have taken a clever man to stop it) the more, in a cross-grained kind of way, it annoyed him. For one thing, he was infuriated by every single remark (and they were frequent enough) made by the staff about Oldroyd's brilliance in thinking of the plan. For another, Mr Braithwaite began to discover that Oldroyd was by no means a genius, and this although his work showed some signs of improvement now that he was not in the same room as Morris. Braithwaite, of course, was intensely jealous of both Morris and Oldroyd. As a man of forty who had been writing advertising copy for twenty-four years, he was jealous of Morris as his senior, although ten years his junior in age; and he was jealous of Oldroyd because he had thought of the biggest idea of the advertising century, and because that fact gave him a privileged position in the copy room, of which Oldroyd for the life of him could hardly help but take advantage. Soon that became a chronic grievance of Braithwaite's. He harped upon Oldroyd's inefficiency at every possible moment, to Oldroyd himself, to Morris, and to Mr Campbell. For one thing, he thought that it displayed the independence of his character not to be overawed by the prestige of the man who thought of the Ultra-violet Bonus Scheme. The unfortunate Oldroyd found that he had gained nothing at all by changing from under Morris's supervision to Braithwaite's.

All the same that young man had drawn moral as well as material benefit from his apparent invention of the scheme. The respect and awe with which the others on the staff regarded him somehow did him good; although he felt that he did not deserve their homage on the grounds on which it was offered, he somehow could not help coming to feel that he deserved it for some reason or other not so apparent. A pound a week rise in salary and a substantial bonus made a difference to him. He could afford slightly better clothes and better food, and a balance of twenty pounds in his newly-opened bank account gave him a solid feeling of security. Moreover, without particularly trying to do so, he had gained a substantial victory over Morris, the man whom he most feared and hated in all the world. Oldroyd really began to feel that he was some-

127

body, and, quite curiously, his walk and gait began to display a jaunty swagger a little reminiscent of Morris's.

And more than that: a little consideration led him to decide to take the offensive against Morris. In accordance with the best tactical theory (although Oldroyd did not think of it like that), having repulsed Morris's attack upon his solid position, he prepared to sally out from his entrenchments and put him utterly to rout, picking up what booty was to be gained during the process. So accustomed had he become to a life of strenuous action and excitement that he felt quite a pleasant anticipatory thrill one day, when he walked across the landing in the office buildings and passed through the door which led into the den of the lion he was about to beard.

In the first room sat Morris's new typist, to whom he nodded familiarly. She could barely afford the time to nod back to him, so hard was she at work for a taskmaster who knew all about the ways of a staff. In the next room was Clarence, in his usual happy position with his legs on his table on each side of his drawing board, contriving even in that impossible attitude to produce neat lettering for Morris's latest ideas for promoting the Bonus Scheme.

'Hullo!' said Clarence.

'Hullo!' said Oldroyd. 'Morris in?'

Clarence wagged his head towards the adjoining room, with its door of frosted glass.

'His lordship's in there,' he said. 'Likewise her ladyship.'

'Miss Campbell, d'you mean?'

'I do, my son. It's quite a usual place for her nowadays.'

'Do you mean to say that—'

'I don't mean to say anything. I'm too clever.'

Oldroyd sat down on Miss Campbell's vacant desk and swung his legs.

'I'll wait then. I don't want to interrupt.'

'I don't know what you want with his lordship, but you stand much more chance of getting it if you don't interrupt, I can tell you,' said Clarence.

Oldroyd did not have to wait long. It was only a short time before the glass door opened and Miss Campbell emerged, papers in hand. She smiled welcomingly on Oldroyd.

'Why, Mr Oldroyd, how are you? I don't get a chance of seeing much of you nowadays, after the move.'

Oldroyd regarded her with an eye which recent experiences

128

had sharpened amazingly, but even his keen glance could detect no sign of guilty innocence in her attitude or demeanour. Nor was there anything for it to detect. Miss Campbell still regarded Morris as no more than her departmental chief. Even if Morris were a much more distinct personality to her than the elegant young men she met socially, he was ages older than her (as she would have said), and he was a married man, and he had manners and an accent which made him quite impossible to her mind. Morris did not realize this in the least. He thought he was making progress.

And he, who had set out to conquer, was fast becoming the conquered. He was finding more and more pleasure in Miss Campbell's company; so much so that that young lady was being called upon to spend much more time at the second table in Morris's private room than at her own in the outer one.

When Oldroyd had exchanged a few casual remarks with Miss Campbell, he rose in leisurely fashion and strolled over to Morris's door.

Although he did not know it, his attitude of imperturbable sang-froid was modelled on what he had seen of Morris's behaviour at other crises. He knocked at the door and entered.

Morris was seated at his desk in the room of which he was so proud. It was furnished as nicely as was Mr Campbell's, with two padded armchairs and an enamelled steel desk, a steel table for a stenographer, a dictaphone and all the other refinements which could give balm to his soul. He frowned when he saw Oldroyd.

'What do you want?' he asked sharply, and that very sharpness in his tone told Oldroyd that Morris was rendered a little anxious at sight of him.

Oldroyd maintained his impassive demeanour. He sat down in one of the padded chairs and crossed his legs.

'Do you mind if I smoke?' he asked – but he asked the question after he had put a cigarette into his mouth and struck a match. The cigarette was alight before Morris could reply.

The two then stared at each other again across the room. Oldroyd was enjoying himself hugely, despite the fact that his impassivity was only a disguise for a fast-beating heart and a lurking nervousness. He could see that Morris was disquietened by his untoward appearance.

'What do you want?' demanded Morris again.

'Lots of things,' said Oldroyd, blowing a cloud of smoke.

'Well, what?'

'I want a quieter life. I want Braithwaite to leave off hazing me. And I want another pound a week.'

'What on earth do you mean?'

'I've said what I mean.'

'If you want to get on the right side of Braithwaite, try doing a bit of work. That's the quickest way. And I'm not the man to come to about a rise in salary. You ought to go to Braithwaite, or Mac – I mean Mr Campbell – if you feel like it. But you're being paid twice what you're worth already.'

'Maybe so. But a word from you to Mac would get me a rise quicker than anything else. And you can arrange something so that Braithwaite can't bother me. I wouldn't mind being transferred here – even although I might intrude sometimes on you and Miss Campbell.'

'What – what—?' stammered Morris.

Oldroyd might have been almost moved to pity for the man if he had not hated him so. The heavy coarse jaw had dropped; there were lines showing obviously about the mouth and eyes. Morris, in fact, was paying heavily for his recent successes. He had more to lose now, and he had begun to worry. This incredible revolt of Oldroyd's left him weak with surprise. He was too astonished at the moment to be angry. Oldroyd's broad hint about Miss Campbell touched him on his weakest spot.

'I don't know what you're talking about,' he said at last. It was only with a fierce effort that he was able to pull himself together to say even that.

'Well, anyway, you know what I want. That's all I wanted to tell you,' said Oldroyd. 'Now you can see that I get it.'

'But you can't do anything to me,' protested Morris. The protest in his tone revealed the fact that he was not too sure of his ground.

'Can't I!' said Oldroyd. 'Don't you think I can? Well, try me, if you like, and see.'

Oldroyd felt quite pleased with himself as he withdrew at that psychological moment. He had not the least idea of what he could do if Morris challenged him to do his worst. But he knew that Morris was anxious about him. And he knew that a man who has committed two murders, and a married man at that, with designs on his employer's daughter, can afford to run no risks whatever. In Oldroyd's shrewd opinion, the time was

130

now past when Morris would dare greatly when a safer and weaker course was open to him.

The man he left behind him in the room behind the glass door may have been of the same opinion at first. Morris, at his desk, sat utterly stunned for a while. It was several minutes before his flamboyant courage came to his rescue. He had faced worse crises than this; he had come through worse dangers. For a moment he was tempted to flout Oldroyd and his threats; to tell the little whipper-snapper to do his very worst and be damned to him. But that was not a course which, on further consideration, made any special appeal to Morris. As Oldroyd had forseen, a threat from an individual possessed of so much knowledge was very efficacious even if it apparently had nothing special to back it up. Morris had heard something about black-mailers. He knew that their demands were ceaseless and increasing. He did not want to dare Oldroyd's threat, but he knew that if he yielded on this occasion he would return shortly with some more impudent demand still. 'Impudent' was the exact word. Morris felt the old working of his rage within him as he thought of Oldroyd's impudence. He hated the fellow, hated him on many more counts than one: for the way he had usurped the credit for Morris's own scheme, for the knowledge he possessed, for the way in which he had foiled Morris's attempt upon him, for this last insolence – even for his wispy moustache and pug nose. A quarter of an hour's meditation brought Morris back to his old condition of furious rage. His fingers, as he sat with his hands on the desk in front of him, writhed and twisted with the thought of brutal physical violence towards Oldroyd. They itched for murder. Morris began to make new plans – plans within plans – for already a new scheme of his which has not yet been mentioned had begun to develop. His imaginative powers had sufficient stimulus now, surely.

# CHAPTER XIX

Although Mr Morris now had a room and a department to himself, it was not at all unusual for him to appear in the old copy room. He had plenty of reasons for coming there, if only (as was the case on this occasion) while waiting for Mr Campbell to finish an interview with a visitor before entering his room to consult with him on some fresh point or other which had arisen. So on that afternoon there was nothing surprising about Morris's entrance into the copy room; no one noticed how keenly he looked about him when he entered, and, as he returned there after the copy room staff had left, no one knew that the first visit had been one in search of something, nor that on the second he had taken away a length of rope, strong and supple, which had come into the office bound round a bundle of samples and had continued to lie for some days under Oldroyd's desk. The natural assumption of anyone in the office, should attention be called to the fact that the rope was missing, would be that Oldroyd had taken it away.

That evening Morris did not go straight home to his wife and family. Seven o'clock found him striding along the twilit streets three miles or so from his home; quite near Oldroyd's lodgings, in fact. His mind was working at double its usual pace, stimulated in part by the pleasant exercise of rapid walking. The intense hatred of Oldroyd which was consuming him did not cloud his judgment; it sharpened it. He ran through detail after detail of the plan he was about to put into action, and he could find no flaw. He fingered, as he walked, the coil of rope in his pocket with fierce delight. He felt a surge of joy throughout his being as he realized that in a few minutes he would be at grips with Oldroyd. It would not be a casual, distant affair, not a shooting or a poisoning or a motorcycle accident, but a fierce clutching of body against body, a desperate physical encounter. Morris's hands opened and shut, and he felt delicious anticipatory thrills at the thought of being at grips with Oldroyd. Although at the same time he must not allow his delight in such an encounter to be over-indulged so as to interfere with the correct arrangement of the circumstantial evidence. Morris might be a madman by now, but he was at least a cunning madman, a daring madman. He was in consequence a hideous menace to society. It is possible that Oldroyd had appreciated this point in a vague sort of way.

Morris looked at his watch. Oldroyd would have finished his supper and would be alone in his room now. Morris felt the noose in his pocket and strode up to the front door. The little servant girl answered his knock, just as she had done months before on the night when Harrison died.

'All right; I know my way,' said Morris, and he had the forethought to give the girl the bold smile which endeared him to servant girls and teashop waitresses. She would not be able to testify to any strangeness in his behaviour on admittance. He held the noose clutched in his left hand within his overcoat pocket as he ran lightly up the stairs. For a man of his bulk he moved with remarkable rapidity and noiselessness – he was taking care to do so. He ran up the stairs to the second floor. Without any obvious haste, and yet without delay, he crossed the landing in a single stride. His right hand gripped the door handle as he did so. He pushed open the door, slipped into the room and shut the door instantly behind him, and even as he closed the door he whipped the noose from out of his pocket.

Oldroyd was sitting beside the gas fire which his rise in salary had procured for him. He was reading the evening paper, and when the door opened suddenly he began to look round to see who was entering so silently and yet so unceremoniously. His eyes lighted upon Morris, huge in his heavy overcoat, and in that instant glance Oldroyd saw upon Morris's face an expression which was horrible to contemplate. Oldroyd had only a fraction of a second in which to contemplate it, for as the door closed behind him Morris drew something from his pocket and leaped silently upon him across the room. Oldroyd had hardly begun to rise from his chair before the noose was about his neck. One of Morris's huge arms was round his chest in a grip of steel, holding both his arms like a vice. The other hand pulled at the noose. Oldroyd felt it tighten. He felt a hideous pain in his throat, while at the same moment Morris, with a madman's display of strength, swung him up from the floor with his single arm and began to bear him across the room – over to the corner where there were hooks screwed to the wall eight feet or more from the floor. Oldroyd's senses swam. Morris's fierce gasping breath in his ear seemed to increase in volume, until it swelled into an enormous noise like the rhythmical beating of an organ. Yet at the same time Oldroyd knew that Morris was being deadly silent, that he was carrying his heavy burden across the room on feet as silent as a tiger's. Oldroyd realized, on the point of unconsciousness, how important was this silence to Morris. Instantly he guessed that his one hope of safety lay in breaking this silence. He struggled in Morris's grip, and his voluntary struggles became more violent as they merged in the spasmodic involuntary writhings of slow suffocation. Even in his agony of pain and fear Oldroyd retained some of his native wits. He made a huge effort to kick over the dressing-table as they went past it, and his toe missed it in a wild upward kick by no more than three inches. He heaved, writhed and struggled in Morris's grasp, while, remorseless as death, Morris bore him steadily over towards those hooks. One hand broke from under Morris's arms and clutched at the bedpost. Morris wrenched and tore to break the grip, but although the bed moved the fingers would not let go. Panting with exertion, Morris tugged and twisted, while Oldroyd's heels hacked at his knees and shins. The fingers would not let go. Morris released his grip of the end of the rope and reached out towards the fingers. A convulsion stronger than any preceding it distorted Oldroyd's body. The fingers quitted the bedpost and shot back, summoned by a wild instinct of self-preservation, to the noose about his neck. They loosened it by the merest, tiniest half-inch. Oldroyd was able to take his first breath since Morris's entrance. It was only a little one, and Oldroyd crowed oddly as he gulped the air, but some went down into his lungs. Then, just as Morris's arm came back to seize the hand which held the noose, Oldroyd was able to save his own life. He screamed, as well as the noose would permit. At first no sound came, but as he writhed and struggled he was able to make some sort of noise. It was a pitiful squeak, like that of a rabbit which has long been in a trap, but it was a piercing noise, and it was maintained for several seconds before Morris could tug anew at the noose and cut it off again.

Morris, with his hand on the rope, stood and hesitated. Someone in the house must have heard that noise; it was penetrating enough. Even if it made no impression now it would be vividly recalled when Oldroyd was found hanging to those hooks. Even the little rumble made when the bed was jerked across the floor might have been heard. That would lead to Morris's death by hanging as well as Oldroyd's, and Morris's life was a thing infinitely more precious than Oldroyd's. Morris was sane enough still to retain the instinct for safety and retreat. The moment after he had pulled the noose tight again he released it once more. More air flooded in to Oldroyd's lungs and his frantic writhings ceased. Morris lowered him to the floor and bent over him.

Oldroyd put both hands to the rope and pulled it loose. Morris had left it amply loose enough for him to breathe, but Oldroyd pulled it looser still. He did not cease until the loop was at least a yard in diameter, the while he breathed deeper and deeper yet, staring up the while at Morris's grim face bent over him. In a new spasm of terror he tried to writhe away from him.

'It's all right now, you fool,' said Morris. 'I'm not going to kill you after all.'

Oldroyd was too busy gulping down air and rubbing his aching throat to make any reply beyond a gasp and a grunt.

Morris regarded him with a complexity of emotions. Disappointment may have been the main one, but he felt very weary and stupid, too. But he felt no sense of defeat. Morris's mentality did not admit that sort of feeling now. He explained the recent failure to himself as a test of circumstances. He had made a trial, and the trial had proved that what he wished to do could not be done; if it could not be done by Morris it was an impossible thing to do. The trial, then, was almost as satisfactory as the success which Morris was sure would come sooner or later. At the same time he thought of an explanation which would maintain his standing in Oldroyd's eyes as a dangerous man, a man to be feared.

'Let that be a lesson to you,' he said. 'If I'd wanted to, you'd be dangling from those hooks now, as dead as a doornail. That'll teach you to meddle with me. Another time I won't let you off.'

Oldroyd goggled up at him from his seat on the floor.

'Behave yourself another time,' said Morris, and he wheeled about and strode from the room.

The sensations experienced in his descent of the stairs were not what he had anticipated earlier in the evening. He had looked forward to leaving a dead man behind him, hanging in that dark corner of the room. It would have been so simple.

135

Braithwaite and the others would have been so ready to bear testimony both to Oldroyd's abstracted behaviour and his recent bad work at the office. He himself would have given evidence that he had called to give Oldroyd very serious warning that dismissal was imminent. The conclusion which any coroner's jury would have reached would be that as soon as Morris had departed Oldroyd had hanged himself in despair. No one at all would have suspected Morris, especially (as Morris guessed) because murder by hanging is the rarest form of homicide known.

It was a pity that the trial had been unsuccessful. It would have been so convenient had it succeeded. Oh, well, another scheme would present itself shortly. Morris did not attempt to think one out as he directed his dragging footsteps homeward. He was feeling very tired.

## CHAPTER XX

Mr Charles Morris, nevertheless, had the right sort of welcome accorded him when he reached home; the kind of welcome a tired man should receive. When his key was heard in the door his wife emerged speedily from the sitting-room and ran to the front door to open it. As he came in she put her hands on his shoulders and kissed his mouth (that heavy, cruel mouth) tenderly. She hung up his hat and helped him off with his coat. Then she led him into the sitting-room. In a twinkling his supper was ready and on the table for him, and she sat beside him and made a pretence of eating with him. Yet at frequent intervals during his meal she put out a thin hand and allowed it to rest on one of his thick ones; then their eyes would meet. There was a world of tenderness in her eyes.

The glance that Morris would give her in return showed no sign of pure or tender passion. It was a sensual bold glare which one would expect of Morris, with all the force of his coarse passion behind it, but it was very pleasant to Mrs Morris. It was long since Morris had looked at her with any passion at all. And after supper Morris rose from the table and, disregarding his wife's pleased expostulations, he carried the dirty crockery out into the scullery and washed it up. It was a very amateurish washing-up; the condition in which he left the sauce-pans would have brought tears to the eyes of a housewife who was not in love with him, but the whole operation was evidently pleasing to his wife. Then, when the washing-up was finished, he came back to the fireside, and Mrs Morris, instead of taking up her customary seat opposite him, pulled her chair round beside him and sat close to him.

They even talked. They even exchanged light gossip. Morris even told Mary a few interesting things about the office – that office which had been a sacred mystery to Mary ever since the days of their honeymoon years before. She listened enraptured. The world was a very pleasant and delectable place to her now that her husband showed in so many ways that he loved her.

That, of course, was exactly the impression which Morris wanted to convey to her. He had been doing this sort of thing for some weeks now, because he wanted his wife to come to believe that he liked nothing so well as her society, that he could never be satiated with it, that hours spent in her company passed as quickly as minutes spent away from her. Morris was clumsy at it. He had no subtlety or delicacy in his actions, but he was successful. He could hardly help but be successful with a lonely woman like Mrs Morris, especially as there was nothing in the world which she wanted so much as the certainty that Charlie loved her – partly because she loved him, and partly because she was possessed of a certain amount of egoism which made attentions to her especially pleasant. It was that egoism which had made a nagging wife of her when Morris neglected her, just as it made a tender, thoughtful wife of her now that he paid her attentions.

The conversation went back and forth around unimportant subjects for a time, Then:

'I met Mrs Herbert this morning while I was shopping,' said Mrs Morris.

'Yes? And what did she have to say?'

'Oh, nothing much. But didn't she look at me though! She wanted me to say something about it, but I wouldn't. Does it show very much, then, Charlie? I didn't think it did.'

'Yes, it does a bit,' said Charlie. 'But not a terrific lot as yet.'

It was rather an understatement. Three pregnancies in quick succession, and none of them properly managed, had made even Mrs Morris's slight figure ungainly and awkward. Her condition was obvious at a glance.

'Oh, dear,' said Mrs Morris. Despite (or perhaps because of) her husband's cautious reply, Mrs Morris guessed at the truth. 'I didn't want it to show so early. The tradespeople do look at one so.'

'Well,' said Morris – this was an opening he had been waiting for for several days – 'well, you've still got time to – you remember what Mrs Whatshername did.'

'Oh, Charlie,' said Mrs Morris, with a world of disappointed reproach in her tone, 'you don't want me to do that; I know you don't. Why, it was only last week you told me – how glad you were.'

She scanned Morris's face anxiously. In his expression there appeared just enough of Morris's actual feelings to make her feel hurt and dejected. She stiffened and broke into rapid speech again.

'No, I'm not going to do that. I'm not going to, Charlie. I don't want to. I told you before I didn't want to. And I'm not going to.'

There were even tears in her eyes, tears of disappointment that this loving husband of hers should be so ignorant of her own wishes.

She was condemning herself to death by those words, but that she did not know. Morris changed his tactics instantly. He had given his wife a fair chance. Up to that moment his new plan of campaign had permitted two possible developments. One – and that the one which, to give him his due, he would have preferred – had come to naught in consequence of his wife's obstinacy. It only remained, therefore, to work on towards the other end – the end being the death of his wife. As consolation, his wife's death, as contrasted with her miscarrying, had the further advantage of permitting him to marry Doris Campbell. At the thought of that a little warm thrill ran through him, and he hastened to erase the bad impression his tentative suggestion had made.

'No,' he said. 'I don't want you to. I don't want you to. I don't want you to do anything you don't want to do. Do just as you like, and that's what I shall like.'

Three weeks ago, before Charlie had begun to woo her again, such a charming speech from her husband might have roused her suspicion. Even as it was she looked at him sharply. But

138

the animal glare of devotion with which he met her eyes suppressed any lurking wonder she may have felt. Even if Charlie, in his heart of hearts, she thought, did not want the child to be born, he was suppressing such a wish in deference to her own desires, and that was more pleasing than ever. She smiled at him and leaned over to him so that her head was on his shoulder. That gave Morris a chance to caress her and quite eradicate any lingering suspicion on her part. When Morris went a-wooing his actions were much more eloquent than his words.

'What about the pictures tomorrow evening?' asked Morris later.

'That would be nice. I was going to ask you, but I was afraid you'd be too tired. There's a talkie at the Hippodrome that I'd like to see. It's called – it's called – I've forgotten what it's called, but I know I wanted to see it. I'll ask Mrs Richmond tomorrow morning if Nellie can come in for the evening.'

Of late, now that Morris had more money to spend, they had begun to pay a girl to sit in the house with the children during evenings when they wished to go out. As a result they had been to the pictures two or three times a week, so that life to Mary Morris, who had hardly been once to a public entertainment since the birth of her first child, was now one long dream of delight. More housekeeping money, a loving husband, and the pictures three times a week – what more could any woman possibly desire? She almost cooed with happiness as she snuggled up to her husband's shoulder.

'Now that the summer's coming in we'll have to get that girl in for the day sometimes on a Sunday, so that we can have the whole day out together,' said Morris. That was the first definite step towards objective number two.

'Ooh!' said Mary. 'Goodness! Where shall we go?'

'Oh,' said Morris, 'out in the country somewhere. We can go on the river. It's years since I've been on the river.'

That was bare truth. Once in his life had Morris gone rowing on the Thames. He had never before to his wife expressed the least yearning for a day in the country with her whether on the river or not. She said as much.

'I didn't know you liked the river, Charlie,' she said.

'Oh, yes, I do,' said Charlie. 'Love it.'

'Where? Kew? Hampton Court?'

Charlie smiled at her pityingly.

139

'You don't know the river like I do,' he said. 'Why, Kew and Hampton Court's nothing to what it is higher up: Maidenhead, where the nobs go. There's Cliveden Reach there, just lovely. And there's Marlow and Windsor and all sorts of places.

With objective number two in mind, Morris had lately been reading a guide-book to the Thames. That was how he knew more about the river than his wife did. Cliveden Reach and Quarry Woods and Bell Weir were no more than names to him either.

'What are they like?' asked his wife.

'Oh, lovely. Big cliffs covered with trees standing up beside the river. Birds singing. And lonely.'

If Mrs Morris had had any cause to suspect him, if she had known as much about Morris as Oldroyd did, for instance, she might have noticed a little change of tone as Morris uttered that last word.

'Lonely,' repeated Morris. He was conscious of that change of tone, and corrected it at the repetition.

'It sounds nice,' said Mary. 'Although we don't have to go and look for lonely places nowadays, do we?'

She laughed happily as she pressed her face against her husband's shoulder. His arm tightened round her instinctively and he kissed her, brutally, as usual, He had no particular desire to kiss her, but he had to maintain appearances, and that was an obvious moment for a kiss. As their lips met together he thought of Doris Campbell and pressed her closer to him. She was perfectly, exquisitely happy. Perhaps these weeks of happiness with a husband who was deliberately plotting her murder would have been considered worth the subsequent tragedy by Mary; certainly it was the happiest time of her life. It was a pity that Morris had not considered it worth while to win the domestic peace and happiness which now were his for the asking without having objective number two solely in his mind. But it never occurred to him to try wooing his wife in this tender fashion save in accordance with a plan; and once Morris had begun to put a plan into practice it never occurred to him that he could leave off. He had to carry it through to the bitter end; that was his nature. It was a dogged characteristic which, however praiseworthy, had very decided disadvantages.

What Morris had suggested came to pass in a few weeks'

140

time, as, of course, was only to be expected. One Sunday morning Mr and Mrs Morris rose early and scanned with anxiety the promise of the heavens. Nellie Richmond arrived to take charge of the children, and Mr and Mrs Morris, after a hurried breakfast, started off, she all a-bubble with excitement, and he, as ever, looking anxiously at his watch and hastening their steps to catch the train.

It was a long, tiring day, and Mrs Morris, if the truth must be told, found it rather exhausting although wholly delightful. They took the train to Charing Cross, and then the tube to Paddington, and at Paddington they just caught the fast train to Maidenhead. From Maidenhead Station it was a long walk to the river, but Mrs Morris did not mind that, for she was too busy looking about her for all the actresses – and worse – who are notoriously accustomed to living in Maidenhead. At the bridge they hired a skiff; a punt was offered to them and refused. Mrs Morris thought that was because her husband had doubts about his punting ability (and loved him for it), but it may have been because punts are so much more stable than skiffs.

Then they started off up-stream, with Morris rowing in lusty windmill fashion and Mrs Morris, in the stern sheets, admiring his prowess and bare forearms, and very pleased that her husband had put on his purple shirt, which showed to such advantage on the river. Boulter's Lock swarmed with craft – skiffs, punts and motor-launches – and the Morris's skiff crashed into several of them under Morris's unskilful handling. Black looks were cast at the pair of them by the occupants of the other boats, Jews and Gentiles, but Mrs Morris merely drew herself up and looked down her nose at them. With her husband present she was not going to be put upon by any la-di-da lot of actresses and their boys.

At last the lock gates opened, and the swarm of boats pressed forward towards Cliveden Reach. Morris's energetic tugs at his sculls took their skiff along well ahead of the punts, and even ahead of most of the skiffs, despite the zigzag course laid down for their boat by Mrs Morris's inexperienced steering. They went on past the weir, and soon the whole vista of the beautiful reach, in broad sunshine, dotted with boats with flannelled crews, was opened up to Mrs Morris's delighted gaze. At her delighted exclamations Morris rested on his sculls and looked over his shoulder; even he was moved by the prospect, although he had to conceal the fact, because he was supposed to have seen Cliveden Reach long before, in the dark, mysterious days before he was married. There are few sights more beautiful than Cliveden Reach on a sunny morning in early summer, with the larks singing overhead and the towering cliffs clothed in their freshest green.

They rowed up to the top of the reach before they stopped for lunch, although by that time it was nearly two o'clock. They moored to the bank, and there Mrs Morris took out their sandwiches from the paper bags, and the cold sausages, and the bananas, and, sitting side by side in the stern seat, they had a delightful picnic lunch, while Morris displayed his purple shirt for the benefit of humanity. Having eaten hugely, they rowed across the river and moored again and, leaving the boat, they landed hurriedly to find beer for Morris. Mrs Morris at the same time drank stout, because she was not very strong just now. Then back again to the shady trees. Morris lay flat on his back in the cushioned seat at the bow, while his wife sat on in the stern and admired the view.

Very few boats had crews energetic enough to row up as far as here; a few went by, and several motor-launches. There were not many people passing to admire Morris's purple shirt. They had this part of the river very much to themselves, despite the fact that it was a fine Sunday. Morris took note of that.

After a long, somnolent interval Mrs Morris opened the paper bags again, and they had tea – more sandwiches, more cold sausages, more bananas. As the sun sank lower Morris put on his coat lest he should catch cold. Then at last Mrs Morris began to grow restless. She began to worry about the house and the children, and after a while she began to voice her restlessness and her fears to her husband. He did not want to go home yet, although his wife timidly reminded him of the long, difficult journey that lay before them. Morris knew of one way in which to silence her arguments and make her forget her fears, and in the end he employed it. He invited his wife to join him in the cushioned seat in the bow, and thither, coyly, she came. They embraced awkwardly with difficulty, lying together in the cramped space. Motor-launches still went by occasionally, but Mrs Morris had no heed for them; with those big arms round her and those kisses on her lips she hardly heeded the passage of time. It was nearly twilight when Morris suggested returning. In the gathering darkness Morris pushed

142

out from the shore and sculled down towards Maidenhead. It was almost dark at Boulter's Lock. It was close on midnight before they reached home, catching the last train from Charing Cross. Mrs Morris was very, very tired. But, beset with the memory of the green countryside and of her husband's kisses, she declared, with all sincerity that it had been the loveliest day of her life.

Morris, too, was well pleased. He had established a splendid precedent. It was one they acted upon repeatedly, Sunday after Sunday, for several Sundays in succession.

## CHAPTER XXI

Oldroyd was not a man given to philosophic meditation on the strangeness of life, which, seeing the situation in which he found himself and the length of time it endured, was as well for him. But sometimes he used his brains, as on the occasion when he had braved all Morris's wrath and won for himself a further rise in salary and a much more comfortable position in the office. These had been announced to him, grudgingly, by Braithwaite at the end of the week following the murderous attempt on Oldroyd's life in Oldroyd's room.

That attempt had shaken Oldroyd badly, but it had not broken his nerve. When Morris had left him, still sitting on the floor with the rope still about his neck, he had taken some time to recover. He had sat there long; for a time the ecstatic delight of being able to breathe freely had occupied his thoughts to the exclusion of everything else, but gradually he had gathered his wits about him and thought the matter out. No matter what Morris had said there was no doubt at all but what his screams had saved his life. Morris would have killed him, have hung him up to those hooks over there, if he had not screamed. That was what Morris had entered to do. Therefore Oldroyd had balked him again, had thwarted even the cunning, powerful Morris, and this for the second time. Oldroyd felt justifiably pleased with himself even at that moment, with his throat hurting him so badly. He knew now that it was a duel to the death with Morris, that it was a question of Morris's life or his own. He disliked the prospect heartily. Perhaps, if he had been given the choice, he would have elected for peace with Morris, but as it was he was determined not to be frightened. He staggered limply to bed, locking his bedroom door for the first time for years, but next morning found him up and weakly prepared to go to the office. A scarf round his neck instead of a collar concealed the bright red weal that the rope had made, and at the same time gave colour to his story of a sore throat, which accounted for the hoarseness of his voice. In this pitiable condition, obviously weak and ill, he appeared in the office. At the very entrance he encountered Morris, who, with his hands in his pockets, was applying his burly shoulder to the swing door. Morris glowered his hatred at Oldroyd: Oldroyd pertly smiled his lack of fear at Morris.

'Remember,' said Oldroyd, his voice hoarse and squeaky by turns, 'remember what I asked for yesterday. I mean it.'

Morris exploded into blasphemy, using foul words, but that morning he went into Mr Campbell and demanded still further reorganization of the office, involving the release of Oldroyd from Braithwaite's supervision, 'so that he could have a chance to think out some more ideas,' Morris weakly explained, which necessitated the addition of still another man to the copy room staff. Apparently as an afterthought, Morris further suggested that Oldroyd should have another rise in salary. Mr Campbell hesitated, but Morris was solid and insistent. So excellent had been Morris's judgment so far that Mr Campbell could not bring himself to go against it. Moreover, the office had ample funds nowadays for the payment of salaries. It could stand for a far bigger increase in the overhead charges than that.

The man who simply could not understand the affair at all was Braithwaite, who vented much ill-temper upon Oldroyd when he announced to Oldroyd that, despite all his, Braithwaite's, recriminations and bad reports, Oldroyd had been promoted, with a rise of salary, to an anomalous position in the office which would take him from under Braithwaite's supervision and make him practically his own master, with no obvious duties whatever. But Oldroyd only smiled at Braithwaite's protestations; he was entering upon the harvest of victory, and he found it very enjoyable.

Later, Mr Campbell saw his bandaged throat and heard his hoarse voice, and sent him home promptly to recover. Mr Campbell forced himself to admit that there must be some good in a young man who would come to the office when he was obviously ill. Oldroyd's bravado had stood him in good stead.

It is hard to describe in writing the effect of all this on Morris. Some people might say Morris was insane; he answered to that description quite aptly in so far as his ideas differed from other people's. His vanity had grown so great now that his two failures to eliminate Oldroyd were quite forgotten as failures. He was determined to destroy him; he had experimented to see whether it was possible without circumstances being in his favour, and had found it impossible. So that all that remained to do was to wait and watch until favourable circumstances arose. In favourable circumstances Harrison had been destroyed; so had Reddy; so, soon, would be his wife. Oldroyd could not hope to stand up long against a man like Morris. That conclusion once reached, Morris regained much of his composure. His intense white-hot hatred of Oldroyd only displayed itself now and again, when Oldroyd was particularly impertinent. Yet he could do nothing, absolutely nothing, without Oldroyd pondering the action and wondering how Morris intended to do him harm by it. And perhaps it is indicative of the fact that Oldroyd was not too sure of his hold over Morris that he should have been saving desperately hard, accumulating quite a respectable balance in his account in readiness for a period of unemployment. And no one in the whole office eyed the burly dark-visaged figure of Morris as he went about the office half as anxiously as Oldroyd did.

For once in a way luck was to turn against Morris. He had had as much good fortune as any criminal could possibly hope for. The killing of Harrison and the killing of Reddy had been achieved in perfectly ideal conditions; every single point had been in favour of him. Now he was to experience misfortune; and, to accentuate the unluckiness of the incident, the misfortune was to be directly due to an attempt on Morris's part to make the preliminaries of his next great scheme as perfect as possible.

Mary Morris had been bewailing the limitations of her wardrobe.

'I've worn that light frock, you know, the one with the blue trimming, for the last three Sundays now. They'll know it when they see it at Boulter's again. And it's the only one that fits me now. It does make me feel awkward among all those smart

145

women at Maidenhead. And I haven't got a proper summer hat.'

'Well, go and get yourself what you want,' said Morris. That showed how fixed was his determination to appear the complete doting husband. 'How much d'you want for a new rigout?'

'Ooh!' said Mary, much impressed. It was the first time she had known Morris volunteer money for her clothing. 'I don't know.'

'Come on,' said Morris; 'out with it.'

'It seems rather a waste,' said Mary, relenting and apologetic. 'A new frock wouldn't fit me very long, and—'

'You could alter it,' said Morris.

'Yes, and I *do* want a new hat. That would last, anyway.'

'Oh, here you are,' said Morris. He pulled out his pocketbook and extracted an astonishing number of pound notes. 'Go and get yourself what you want.'

Mary contemplated the huge sum with astonished eyes.

'That *is* lovely, darling,' she said. 'But – but – are you sure you can afford it!'

'No,' grinned Morris, 'of course I can't with an extravagant wife like you. Here, take it.'

'I could buy a nice frock and hat up West with this,' marvelled Mary.

'Well, why don't you?'

'I think I will. And shall I come into the office for you afterwards?'

'No,' said Morris sharply. That had taken him by surprise. He did not want Miss Campbell to see his wife, especially in her present condition.

Mary may have noticed the sharpness of his tone, for she swallowed her disappointment and said no more. But it may have influenced her future actions.

So it came to pass that Oldroyd, wandering one afternoon into the teashop near the office for a cup of tea, heard a voice call his name just as he was about to descend the stairs to the smoke-room. Mrs Morris, encumbered with parcels, was sitting at a table beside the stairs.

'It's Mr Oldroyd, isn't it?' she said. It seems quite certain that she had chosen that particular teashop for her tea in the hope or fear of seeing her husband there.

'Yes, why you're Mrs Morris, aren't you?' said Oldroyd.

146

'Oh, you ought to know me,' replied Mrs Morris playfully; 'we've seen each other often enough before.'

So they had, in the old days, when Morris and Oldroyd were friends.

'Won't you sit here, or are you expecting anyone?' said Mrs Morris. That was one good service her husband's new attentions had done her; they had given her a self-assurance and poise which she had lacked before in her encounters with the opposite sex.

'Thank you,' said Oldroyd, and sat down.

He looked at Mrs Morris in rather puzzled fashion. He was wondering whether this chance encounter was part of some new deep scheme on the part of Morris. But he decided that it was not. Not even Morris could find a use for Mrs Morris in any criminal plan.

'Dreadfully hot, isn't it?' said Mrs Morris. 'And it's been so tiring shopping in town.'

She indicated all the numerous parcels beside her.

'I suppose so,' said Oldroyd.

'I've had to buy such a lot of new things for the river,' said Mrs Morris.

'For the river?' Oldroyd's eyebrows went up a little; his attention was caught.

'Yes,' said Mrs Morris.

She took much pleasure in telling everyone she met about her frequent trips on the river with her adoring husband, which was just what her adoring husband wanted her to do.

'We go on the river every week now,' went on Mrs Morris. 'Charlie used to go such a lot before he was married, and now the children are old enough to be left with a maid it's so nice for him to go again.'

'Yes, of course,' said Oldroyd. This was all intensely interesting, because he had known Morris quite well before he was married, and this was the first he had heard about a passion for going on the river.

'Every Sunday we go,' said Mary proudly. 'Of course, it's rather a long way, but it's so nice when we get there.'

'I suppose it is,' said Oldroyd. 'Where do you go?'

'Maidenhead,' replied Mrs Morris. It was lovely to talk about 'Maidenhead' in this casual, opulent fashion. 'Charlie loves Cliveden Reach so much. We catch the 9.55 at Paddington, and we have our dinner and tea on the water. It's quite

147

late – in fact, it's nearly dark – before we come back again.'

'That must be nice,' said Oldroyd.

Clearly there was nothing in all this which meant danger to him as long as he was not invited to be one of the party. But – but – there was danger to someone else, or he did not know Morris as well as he thought he did. He was puzzled. He had formed the egotistical habit of thinking that he alone formed the important part of Morris's small world.

'I suppose you two go alone every time?' he asked casually.

'Of course,' said Mrs Morris, as if that was the only possible way for them to go.

That 'of course' opened Oldroyd's eyes still wider, and when they opened wider Mrs Morris actually blushed. So Morris was making love to his wife. That was a strange thing for him to do. Oldroyd's suspicions grew stronger and stronger. It was astonishing, too, how keen his danger and suspicions were making his wits.

'It must be jolly nice,' said Oldroyd again. His conversational powers were not specially distinguished.

Yet he would have liked to go on talking had he not been interrupted by Mrs Morris looking at the clock and rising to go.

'Good-bye,' she said. 'You must come round and see us some time. I don't know why you've left off coming.'

Then she turned to go, and in that instant Oldroyd noticed something else. He was not a very domesticated young man, nor was he used to women, but there was that about Mrs Morris which not even Oldroyd could help noticing when she stood up. He had more now to think about than ever.


## CHAPTER XXII


During the rest of the week, up to the week-end, Oldroyd's slow mind was working on a certain limited amount of data, and endeavouring to discover more. Morris had suddenly adopted a new and unusual habit. That in itself was suspicious. Certain of the details of the habit were also suspicious – the going always to the same place and the staying unusually late.

If Morris's new love for the river was genuine, why did he always choose Cliveden Reach when there were plenty of places more accessible? It was quite a while before Oldroyd decided that it must be because he wanted to form a series of precedents, so that on some special day in the future there would be no comment made. But what was he meditating to do on that special day? Even Oldroyd's slow mind jumped to the conclusion that he intended murdering his wife; but that seemed at first so motiveless that Oldroyd could not bring himself to believe it. But conviction came slowly. There was enough whispered office gossip about Morris's passion for Miss Campbell to make it seem likely. Then – then – Oldroyd knew that Mrs Morris's condition might supply quite a deal of additional motive; in the old days Morris had often expressed himself forcibly to Oldroyd on the subject of 'kids'. Oldroyd was not a man of acute psychological insight; quite on the contrary. But his recent adventures and his deadly fear and hatred of Morris were a sufficient spur to goad him into achieving a neat piece of deduction; he pierced Morris's design almost

But it was not enough to have done so much, to treat it as a purely academic problem. For thirty-six hours Oldroyd was haunted by indecision as to what he ought to do next. He shrank with repulsion from the possibility that he could wash his hands of the whole business and leave Morris a free hand to accomplish his design. Oldroyd had a prejudice (which Morris might have thought odd) against murder, even when he was not the destined victim. He hated the thought of little Mrs Morris being done to death by her hairy brute of a husband. Yet, as he asked himself persistently, what was there he could do? The police would hoot with laughter if he went to them and said that his fellow-clerk had taken to going on the river with his wife and therefore was plotting her murder. They would listen with more attention if he went on to say what else he knew of Morris, but that he could not do without betraying himself. Despite his bold words to Morris and his comforting repetition to himself of the convenient phrase 'King's Evidence', he did not want to involve himself in such a fashion.

The little Yorkshireman gnawed at his nails and worried his silly little moustache as he tried to reach a decision. It is saying much for him that he eventually decided that he would make the sacrifice and go to the police if he could not think of any other method of saving Mrs Morris's life. All the same, before doing so, he started to probe all the other possibilities open to him.

There was something else he could do, after all, he decided. it would mean pitting his wits and his strength against Morris's, and possibly entangling himself in an unsavoury business. But the entanglement would be nothing compared with the alternative of going to the police, and so could be ruled out. It was far harder to decide to face Morris in all his wrath and his strength. Morris inspired his enemies with very definite feelings of fear and repulsion. Oldroyd's eventual decision to match himself against Morris in the fashion he foresaw was nothing short of heroic, whatever the arguments to the contrary which might be advanced. Two successful encounters with Morris might have given him self-confidence. He might be spoiling for a fight with the enemy who sought his death so ruthlessly. But for all that, little Oldroyd, when he left off biting his nails and shut his fists instead, and when he announced to his vacant bedroom, 'I'll do it, too, by gum!' was being brave enough to justify quite a large amount of pride in his own conduct. He felt none at all, of course. He set himself, instead, to the un-usually difficult task, for him, of trying to plan out all his actions for the morrow (which was Sunday) and to visualize those of Morris and his wife.

And such was his care and prevision that everything went off without a hitch. Early the next morning found him at Paddington Station, where he was the first person through the barriers and on to the platform where the 9.55 to Maidenhead was waiting. He did not enter the train immediately. He hurried down to the very farthest end of the platform and hid himself inconspicuously behind a mass of baggage. There he waited patiently until he saw Morris and his wife coming down the platform towards him. There was no mistaking Morris's big body and rapid walk. Oldroyd, as he watched him, marvelled at his assurance of bearing. He quite dwarfed Mrs Morris, who trotted along at his side, with feelings of mingled delight in her new frock and shame at the conspicuousness of her figure. Morris opened a carriage door, and the two climbed in! Oldroyd in his turn waited until the train was almost due to start before he walked back and entered a carriage near the engine, so that he would not have to pass Morris's carriage door.

150

At Maidenhead Station he lingered again in the train until it was almost due to go out again. Then he lingered further on the platform. Eventually the other two had quite a long start on him on their way to the river. They had hired their skiff and were well on their way to Boulter's Lock before Oldroyd reached the riverside. There he hired a dinghy and sculled slowly after them.

He passed the lock in the batch behind them; by the time he emerged Morris's energetic sculling had taken them up round the bend, but Oldroyd pulled stubbornly after them, upstream. Cautiously looking over his shoulder from time to time, he caught sight of them at last, moored beneath the trees at the very head of the reach, almost at Cookham, and when he had them well in view he, too, pulled into the bank and moored, where willows screened him, in one of those little niches where lovers have moored since time immemorial. Peering out through the willows he had the skiff well in view, and so he set himself to wait, with uncomplaining patience, until the end of the day.

One thing only had Oldroyd forgotten in his plans for the day, and that was food for himself. But his native stubbornness came to his rescue. He bore the pangs of hunger and thirst and inactivity for hour after hour, as noon changed to afternoon, and afternoon to evening. There was heroism in that, too, for Oldroyd had strong ideas on the subject of the correct treatment of his interior.

Worst of all, on this day all his trouble and care and patience were wasted; Morris did nothing that day which contravened the law. At nightfall he untied his skiff and rowed back down the river, past Oldroyd behind the screen of willows, and on to Boulter's Lock. Oldroyd, following immediately they had passed, had to wait for them to pass the lock first, and in consequence he delivered back his dinghy to a very impatient and irate boat hirer. Moreover, he only just caught his train back to London, although he was lucky in avoiding Morris's eye in the seething weekend crowd on the platform. Oldroyd reached his lodgings at midnight, very tired, very exasperated and, worst of all, very hungry – and, of course, there was no food accessible to him.

After an experience like that Oldroyd might have been fully justified in abandoning his plan. He could so easily have come to the conclusion that he was wrong, that Morris meditated no harm, and that there was no need to continue to go to this incredible amount of trouble. It would have been an easy, comfortable course to take. But Oldroyd had more courage; he had the courage of his convictions, although the scoffer may sneer that it was, instead, only pigheaded obstinacy. He reasoned with himself that Morris had gone on the river three or four times already in his careful arranging of a series of precedents, and that there was no reason whatever that he should have timed the 'accident' he had in mind for the first occasion when Oldroyd followed him. Morris, Oldroyd knew, would act with cunning and caution, and only when he was certain that the time was ripe.

Yet, all the same, Oldroyd was worried and anxious. He was not at all sure what Morris's plan actually was, or even whether he really had a plan. And possibly – now that Oldroyd had time to think this kind of fear came readily enough – that plan might be more subtle than Oldroyd was counting on. It might actually be directed against Oldroyd himself; that meeting with Mrs Morris in the teashop *might* not have been so accidental as it appeared. Morris was quite capable, to Oldroyd's mind, of plotting the whole thing so as to lure Oldroyd on to the river with him, so that the next time Oldroyd followed them he might find himself in the grip of the tiger's claws. He would be found drowned later, the victim of one more deplorable accident. Oldroyd did not miss the possibility, which shows how acute his wits were becoming, but he shrugged his shoulders at it, metaphorically speaking. He would face Morris in his rage as he had faced him before. Next Sunday would perhaps solve the question for him; until then he could bear to wait. But the waiting seemed long to Oldroyd, all the same, and he looked at Morris more and more anxiously as the week went by when he met him in the office.

And so next Sunday morning found Oldroyd once more the first to enter upon the platform of the 9.55 Paddington to Maidenhead. Once more he saw Morris stride, and Mrs Morris trot, up the platform. Once more he slunk behind them to the riverside and, hiring his dinghy, pursued them up the length of Cliveden Reach. The friendly willow was still there, and in exactly the right position to overlook the couple as they rested moored to the bank. Oldroyd settled himself for another long period of waiting.

Today, with more foresight, he had brought food and drink

with him, but today, curiously enough, he felt neither appetite nor thirst. His throat felt constricted with excitement. He felt a powerful premonition, which had not been at all apparent the week before, that today would bring with it the crucial development. He could not eat, nor drink, but spent the long, weary afternoon and evening moving restlessly about the dinghy, parting the branches of the willows every two minutes to see that all was well in the skiff.

So that it was with a dull feeling of disappointment that, when night fell, he heard the clatter of sculls being put into the rowlocks, and the dip of the blades. Then the skiff came slowly past him, heading downstream. Looking out from under the willow, he saw Morris's heavy profile clearly outlined against the pale sky. He heard him make some remark in a low voice to his wife, and he heard her reply. Oldroyd, crouched in his boat, realized at that moment the nightmare character of the whole affair. For a space he began to doubt not merely himself and his own sanity, but the very occurrence of the incidents of the last six months. He felt he could not believe that Harrison had died by Morris's hand, or that Reddy had met his death otherwise than by accident. He even began to doubt whether Morris had twice tried to kill him. Certainly he could not believe that Morris was planning to kill his wife. Then he remembered how his throat had pained him one evening after a surprise visit from Morris, and he shook himself back to reality.

Still at the back of his mind, as he untied the painter and pushed out into midstream, there was a half-formed decision not to repeat this ridiculous business of shadowing again. Looking back down the river he saw, two hundred yards downstream, a small black shape on the surface of the water. That was Morris's skiff. He leaned forward to take a few gentle strokes with his sculls in pursuit.

Then, before the stroke could be completed, he heard something which caused him to throw all his strength upon his sculls, so quickly did the tenseness of his nerves cause him to react. From the black shape downstream there came a scream and a splash. As Oldroyd sent the dinghy flying down to the skiff he heard another scream which was choked half-way through in an ugly, bubbling fashion.

The state of mind of a murderer at the instant of his crime is something hard to imagine, but Oldroyd was offered some

153

insight into it when his dinghy had covered the gap between it and the skiff. The latter was floating bottom upwards. All round it were floating dark lines and masses – cushions, sculls and boathook. Beside the skiff was something paler in hue – Morris's face. Oldroyd caught a glimpse of it in the faint light as the dinghy came surging up. The brows were set in a frown of horrible intensity; the jaw was locked in an expression of furious determination. Morris was treading water, and he had his arms outstretched to his wife, whose white dress was just visible in the black water. A casual excited glance might have thought he was trying to hold her up, but instead Morris was pushing her down under the surface.

So intent had Morris been on his task that he had not heard the swirl of the water under the bows of the dinghy as it came rushing up, while Oldroyd, scull in hand, sprang to his feet to see what he could do. Morris caught sight of Oldroyd; he may even have recognized him in that faint light, for his expression changed to one of intense malice and rage. But Oldroyd did not stop to look or inquire. The scull was in his hand. All his hatred and fear and loathing found vent as he reversed his grip on it and swung the butt with all his strength upon Morris's head. It struck with a dull crash and Morris relaxed his grip on his wife and sank, inert and limp, below the water. Oldroyd suddenly found himself trembling and weak as he stood in the swaying boat.

So the career of Morris was ended. For months now he had opposed himself to the law, and it was not the law which defeated him. On those grounds Morris might claim posthumously a highly successful criminal record. All the machinery of society, all the thousands of police, the majesty of law, the last awful threat of the gallows had been successfully defied. It was instead by the vigour and courage of a private individual that he had been thwarted at last. But that, of course, would have been only the very poorest consolation to Morris.

His body lay at the bottom of the river, bumping gently over the gravel as the current took it very slowly downstream, rolling it over and over with languid movements, down to where the rushing weir of Boulter's Lock awaited it, where the posts and piles and torrential stream effectually erased all sign of what Oldroyd's oar had done to its head. Everyone was sorry that a deplorable accident had deprived the world of a most forceful and efficient member of society, who had bade fair to rise to the greatest distinction. Save perhaps Oldroyd, and possibly Mrs Morris, who, despite all that Oldroyd could say, could never afterwards quite believe that the fierce hands which had held her so mercilessly under water had really been trying to save her and not to drown her.

Oldroyd, still trembling, had noticed a gleam of white below the surface of the water; he had reached down and found Mrs Morris's unconscious body floating there; enough air had remained in her clothes to keep her half afloat when her husband sank. Somehow Oldroyd pulled her out, and prompt measures at My Lady Ferry had brought her back to life.

So that even Morris's great record proved on analysis to be nothing to boast about. His two great successes are balanced by three utter failures, while no one can deny that he had been amazingly favoured by fortune. Certainly Oldroyd felt no inducement whatever to follow his example; he remains satisfied with having committed one murder and with having been accessory to another. The coroner's jury which investigated Morris's death saw fit to congratulate Oldroyd on his very prompt rescue of Mrs Morris, and quite understood that in the darkness his failure to save Morris as well was perfectly excusable. And they added a very valuable rider to the verdict which commented on the danger of changing seats in a skiff in the middle of the river.

# Payment Deferred

William Marble couldn't understand how he had got into such
debt. His home was modest – seedy, some might say – and his
way of life unpretentious. Not that he was tight-fisted. There
was his photography – but a man has to have a hobby. As for
his fondness for whiskey, what was life if a fellow couldn't
take a drink?

Still, the bank he worked for wouldn't see things that way:
his appearance in the bankruptcy court would mean certain
dismissal. For a man like Marble that was enough to sanction
murder. Murder that would sort out all his money problems
at a trifling cost.

But there is always a price to be paid for taking human life,
and the bill may be presented when least expected. When that
happened, there would be no credit for William Marble . . .

Gripping from its macabre opening to its final, undivinable
twist, *Payment Deferred* established C. S. Forester as a
bestselling author. With *Plain Murder*, it is proof that the
creator of Hornblower also ranks among the great crime
novelists of this century.

80p

# Brown on Resolution

In the autumn of 1914, the nations of Europe are already locked in a bloody stalemate. But thousands of miles away, on the remote Pacific island of Resolution, a different, and very personal, battle is about to begin.

High among the island's volcanic crags, a young English sailor gazes down on the German raider *Ziethen*, the battle-cruiser whose guns had sunk his ship and sent his crewmates to their deaths. Armed only with a stolen rifle and stubborn, unquestioning courage, Leading Seaman Albert Brown is determined to stop *Ziethen* from making herself seaworthy and leaving Resolution before the searching British navy arrives. Even if it costs his twenty-year-old life . . .

*Brown on Resolution* is an epic tale of individual courage in war, one of the incomparable C. S. Forester's most stirring story-telling achievements.

60p

# Death to the French

1810. Napoleon's last great advance into Portugal has forced the British under Wellington back on the line of the Torres Vedras, to make their stand with Lisbon and the sea behind them.

But for one British soldier, Rifleman Dodd of the Ninety-Fifth, there is no retreat. Cut off from his comrades by the enemy's advance, he finds himself alone in French-held territory.

Dodd survives – and, with a combination of rough resourcefulness and dogged courage, succeeds in welding a band of ragged, undisciplined Portuguese guerrillas into a brutally effective fighting-force, an instrument for his own private war against the might of France.

Death to the French is one of this master story-teller's greatest achievements: both a thrilling classic of individual adventure and a vivid re-creation of a fascinating episode in the history of warfare.

60p

# The Gun

Abandoned by the retreating Spanish army during the Peninsular War, the gun was a magnificent eighteen-pounder, thirteen foot long, three tons of bronze emblazoned with heraldic tracery. Rescued and remounted by a Spanish guerrilla band, it became the focus of the ever-swelling numbers of Spanish irregulars, battering great fortresses into submission and destroying the cream of Napoleon's troops. The gun was a powerful object of pride and reverence to the Spanish. To the French it spelled wholesale destruction . . .

*The Gun* is one of C. S. Forester's most famous stories, and was filmed under the title *The Pride and the Passion*. Sir Hugh Walpole described it together with *Death to the French* as 'His best works . . . these two military episodes are remarkable for their vividness and commonsense. He writes like an eyewitness.'

95p

## C. S. Forester in Triad/Mayflower Books